Refugee

Refugee

ANNE ROSE

The Dial Press
New York

Printed in the United States of America
Printed and bound by Vail-Ballou Press, Inc.
First Printing
Design by Atha Tehon

Library of Congress Cataloging in Publication Data
Rose, Anne K
Refugee.
Summary: Traces a twelve-year-old Jewish girl's
flight from Belgium prior to Hitler's invasion
and her life in New York until the age
of eighteen when the war ends.
[1. Jews—Fiction   2. World War, 1939–1949
—Refugees—Fiction]   I. Title.
PZ7.R7144Re   [Fic]   77-71519
ISBN 0-8037-7285-8

To G— and L—
In memory

Refugee

Antwerp, October 12, 1939

I don't like Mme. Pinot, I hate her. We all hate her. Ever since she arrived to replace our Flemish principal we have to speak French in class. It's always back and forth here in Belgium, the Flemings and Walloons fighting each other. Antwerp is the capital of Flanders and we speak Flemish, of course, but now that the Walloons are in power our classes have shifted to French.

Mme. Pinot is Walloon. As if that isn't enough, we have inspection twice a week now. Mondays and Thursdays Mme. Pinot examines our heads with a thin fine louse comb.

Close up her face is a map of tiny red rivers running toward a wide purple sea, her nose. Above the purple nose pale eyes bulge furious. No matter how hard I scrub I'm never sure how clean my scalp is going to look to those watery eyes. Nobody in class is.

Mme. Pinot checks our fingernails too. No cosmetics of any sort are allowed. L'Athénée Royale pour Jeunes Filles is a school for girls through age sixteen and is very strict. I am twelve-and-a-half.

I don't like to show my bitten nails to the principal, and I don't like to bow my head to her when we file out of school either, and mostly I don't, but my heart pounds hard in my throat when her eyes bulge out at me then.

Mme. Hachette, our Latin teacher, is Walloon too. She has eyes in the back of her head and there's no way we can hide from her. Once I poured glue on her seat. I stuck velvet flowers from one of my mother's old hats all around to make it beautiful, but she still didn't like it.

That was back last May. Then spring burst with red poppies all over and we forgot about Walloon trouble, and besides, French is nice, and so I celebrated by showering colored confetti all over our algebra teacher. It was then that Papa was called in to Mme. Pinot's office.

"I have six hundred pupils in this school," she told him sternly, "but your daughter Elke makes more trouble for me than the other five hundred ninety-nine others put together."

I felt proud when I heard Papa tell Maman about it. Even though it was bad that Papa had to see the principal because of the algebra teacher, I was a celebrity in school now. The song I had made up for the confetti dance was especially fine, I thought. It went like this:

Vive les vacances, vive les vacances
Tous les livres aux feux
Et la demoiselle au milieu!

Hurray for vacations! Hurray for vacations!
Throw the schoolbooks into the fire,
And the teacher, add her to the pyre!

All my friends admired it a lot, but Papa and Maman didn't. They didn't care for the confetti either, it seems, because I was grounded for a whole month after Papa's visit to Mme. Pinot. That's when I decided to begin this secret diary, when I was grounded.

Antwerp, October 19, 1939

The bell! I thought it would never ring today, after Latin and gym and algebra and that long history lesson. We're doing Flanders under the Spanish occupation of the Duke of Alba. He's the one in all the oil paintings, the duke with the long thin nose and the starched collar. He was a mean one, Alba was, the worst tyrant we had until the Germans overran Belgium in the Great War of 1914–1918, my teacher says.

But that happened so long ago, it's boring. Dates blur in my dusty history book and my fingers are inky from so much scribbling. School is from eight to five every day but Wednesday, when there's piano and ballet, and on Saturday there are classes till noon. Summer vacation isn't till July 21st, Belgian Independence Day, and that seems so very far away.

It's a crisp autumn day. Ginna, Lara, and I kick chestnuts to each other on the way home for the big midday meal. This isn't as easy as it sounds; chestnuts have a silly habit of rolling under cobblestones and getting stuck, making you lose the game. After a time we switch and pull doorbells for fun. We ring and run, run fast in the wind, the red and brown fall leaves blowing in our laughing faces.

The blue stoops in front of all the houses have been freshly scrubbed for the day. Everybody's safely inside eating the main meal now and we have the streets to ourselves as we run. Two whole hours of freedom until the school's iron gate shuts us in again until dark!

A crowd has gathered farther up on the street by the corner of the park. Another parade, most likely. I love marching parades with drums and trumpets and people in bright costumes. The beat is so much more brisk than in those slow solemn Catholic processions we have for every saint on the calendar here. Like the one last week. Church bells tolled as drummers marched down the street, heavy with gloom and doom. Everyone crossed themselves and knelt, everyone but me that is, and not kneeling is as bad as not bowing to the principal, worse even. I felt funny inside me, being Jewish at a Catholic procession, and sort of scared, too. I wished Ginna and Lara were with me. There would have been three of us not kneeling then, and my stomach wouldn't have cramped up from being alone like that.

Today the group of people is not lined along the road the way it usually is but stands clustered together, tight as a fist. It is not a Catholic procession or a marching parade, it seems.

The bunched crowd isn't costumed, I see now, they aren't wearing uniforms of any sort, except boots. They are dressed like anybody else but look different; they look like cutthroats with their black shiny boots and closed faces. Some of them wear shiny emblems on their lapels, the twisted-cross swastikas of the Flemish Nazi party.

We move up, a little slower than before, shuffling closer to the silent mob. A cold feeling grips me though I'm not cold, not cold at all, sweating a little really.

There are no drums or trumpets, only silence torn by laughter. The nasty hooting kind that boys drowning a cat for fun laugh.

But the thugs aren't drowning a cat, they're doing something else. They are amusing themselves by humiliating an old Jewish man. The old man is collecting garbage the Nazis have kicked over with their boots.

He stoops and picks and his hat falls off. The hoods jeer, their clubs tight in their fists. They are making the old man pick garbage to make him feel like refuse, I think. He picks and picks in a great hurry, but not fast enough for them.

"Quicker, quicker, before the police get here!" they shout, prodding him on with their clubs and calling him ugly names.

But the old man has stopped. He lifts his head and

stares at them, not budging at all now. Suddenly he looks like my grandfather used to look—frail, breakable, yet hard somehow.

Sirens! Police cars screech around the corner, and the Nazis scurry away for safety, vanishing in the park's shadows.

Antwerp, October 24, 1939

Black bats flap danger in the dark. I cry out in my nightmare, but in the morning I remember nothing.

"But something did happen at the street corner," Maman reminds me. "They did bully that old man. That sort of thing is happening more and more. No, no, we aren't safe in Europe any longer." Her eyes glitter in her flushed face. "These are dangerous times, *sauve-qui-peut* times. It's save-whoever-can-be-saved now."

Papa, too, says things look bad. The Flemish Nazis are growing in numbers and are noisy with their new-found power. England and France are at war with Hitler now but the Germans have snatched up Poland and Czechoslovakia without a battle. It's only a matter of months—who knows, weeks—before they invade us as they did in the War of 1914–1918.

These are strange, dreamlike days. Though we haven't been bombed yet, we have daily gas-mask drills at school now. Stories about mustard gas and other poison gases used in the Great War are scaring us to line up for masks. After we got them we made monster sounds to go with the monster faces we now wore, but nobody laughed.

Mevrouw Hoog next door cannot get a mask small enough to fit her baby. She was told to soak a diaper in urine and hold it against his face during an air attack. The ammonia in the urine will keep the gas out, she was assured, but she looks worried still.

My best friend Ginna's older brother Maurice is in the army. Piet across the street is too, and so is Mynheer Hoog and Papa's young cousins Léon and Albert. Papa himself is too old for the service—he is forty-eight—but most other men are not around anymore. The boys who deliver coal are gone, as are the pink-faced country boys who bring the milk and butter. Old men, sometimes even old women, do their work these days. Even the lamplighter who comes around at dusk has been drafted and our neighbor Frans lights the lamps for him now. Frans is only twenty but Frans is a special case. He limps from a wound he got as a volunteer in Spain's Civil War and the army won't have him.

The city is dark after nine, with dim blue lights spooking things up here and there, and the streets are deserted. But by day Antwerp is alive with all sorts of new people, refugees from foreign lands and our own soldiers among them.

The soldiers clog the streets doing nothing, but it's sort of fun having them here. Joking, smoking, they cluster at corners swapping stories and calling to the passing girls.

I like the general mobilization. There, I said it! I like seeing so many boys in rough green-wool uniforms. They all look like movie heroes. And they say things that make me feel like I'm in the movies too.

But the grown-ups don't feel that way at all. The grown-ups are nervous. Things cost more all the time and soon they won't be available at all, they say, and so they buy more and that makes the prices go up and that makes them more nervous still; it is the war of nerves. Some call it the phony war.

On top of everything Uncle Jacques, Maman's brother in America, keeps wiring telegrams that shout TIME RUNNING OUT: ACT NOW! and BETTER SAFE THAN SORRY! and LATER WILL BE TOO LATE!

Antwerp, November 5, 1939

Something big and terrible is about to happen yet I'm sort of feverish with excitement, like before an exam or a big adventure or something.

I daydream a lot now. Bombs are dropping all over Antwerp. I'm hit, my leg's cut and swelling, my face is bleeding. The pain is awful, yet I stay to bandage the wounded alongside a handsome young doctor whose adoring Valentino eyes are on me while I work.

The bombs have set my school on fire. Dragging my wounded leg I dash through the flames. Mme. Pinot lies gasping for breath in her burning office. As I pull her out to safety she whispers, "Of all my six hundred pupils you're the very finest," and faints in my arms.

"In these *sauve-qui-peut* times you're lucky, Elke," Maman says, interrupting my daydream. She smiles a weak smile. "You've always been lucky, remember that. You can get papers for America!"

"Lucky," I shout. "What's lucky about that?"

I'm not afraid of bombs and war—I'll never die. I'll never get old, either. I pinch my skin to wrinkle it, but it springs back as smooth and pink as before.

Somewhere, though, I know she's right. Hitler's on the front page all the time now. Hitler shaking hands with Mussolini, Daladier, Chamberlain; Hitler reviewing his troops; Hitler addressing mass rallies. We hear his hoarse, frantic voice whipping up German mobs to glass-shattering frenzy and I think of the *Kristallnacht*, the terrible "Night of Broken Glass" when Jewish shop windows all over Germany were smashed and their owners beaten and dragged off to concentration camps. I've heard Papa and Maman talk about concentration camps, but the moment I'm around they stop talking so I know they must be bad.

More and more people are crossing into Belgium to escape from Hitler Germany now. Many of them look rich, but they can't be because they wait in the soup lines at the Charité Centrale where Maman helps out. Belgian law does not permit foreigners to work here, so all they can do is stand around and smoke nervously, just as our own soldiers do. But what they talk about is different.

"Evil has been unleashed! The Nazis are taking the world over and we are letting them!" a German refugee on a soapbox shouts, his voice thick with warning. "Listen! Unless we fight back we Jews will all end up as their slaves!"

Ginna and I listen with round eyes to the prophet on the soapbox. "Mark my words, my friends," he roars, "and mark them carefully: They mean it when they call themselves the Master Race, and they mean to make it happen!"

We jump on our bikes and ride away fast, the wind in our hair. We don't want to hear that awful man on the soapbox with that awful, frightened look on his face. We don't even want to think about it, it's too scary.

Antwerp, November 12, 1939

"Lucky indeed," I mutter, slamming the door behind me in protest. "I don't want to leave, I want to stay here with you!"

Just the same I have to go to the American consulate. I don't want to, but my parents say I must.

Papa and Maman have been knocking on the consul's door with no success. It seems the papers they have are the wrong ones for the papers they need. It's not that the United States does not want Maman and Papa, the American consul explained patiently, it's that America needs West European immigrants more than East European immigrants. America already has too many of the other kind, the Austrian East European kind Maman and Papa happen to be. This is called the "quota system" it seems.

It was then that Maman said, "Elke here was born in the right place at the right time so we'll send her. These are hard times, times to save whoever can be saved."

It was after that that she said, "You've always been lucky, Elleke."

But I don't feel lucky. To be lucky is to win the lottery or to be beautiful like a princess, but I'm not. I'm sort of a skinny weed with plain straight hair. Some of my friends already wear bras but I'm still like a boy on top and I don't call that lucky.

I want to stay home and be with everybody else but now I have to leave. I've been singled out in a way I don't like at all and I'm supposed to feel lucky.

I grew up here on these crooked cobbled streets with narrow houses and funny roofs that zigzag like ladders up to the sky. I don't want to leave what I love for a strange cold place. I'm warm here.

"You don't understand, child," Maman says.

Maman is right. I don't understand.

Antwerp, November 13, 1939

Ginna is my best friend. She's plump and giddy, and we laugh all the time, she and I. Everything about her is jolly, her brown eyes with the dancing green flecks in them, her shiny white teeth, the dimples in her plum-colored cheeks.

She hates the way she looks though. Her thighs are too full, she says, her rear too round. We're self-critical like that, all of us, even Lara. We have long sessions on how to swap parts to create the perfect beauty specimen. It's our favorite game when it's too cold out for biking around town.

Ginna always smells good from all the samples around her home. Her father is a perfumer. He works with the essences of musk and roses, among others, and Ginna seems to carry a scent of spring with her everywhere she is.

Or did. Her house is different since her father lost his post as chemist-perfumer with the big company whose headquarters are in Hamburg, Germany. They fired him because he is Jewish. Ginna said he offered to change his name from Werner to Wotan to give it that pure Viking-Aryan-Nazi sound, but he still couldn't keep his job.

The Werners opened a corner pub after a time. Beer and sausages can be had there, and small pastries and Belgian *café-filtre* too. Mrs. Werner looks tired from all the baking she does, but the house smells of butter and cinnamon, which is better than the aroma of fine perfumes anytime, but that's easy for me to say.

Now Ginna has to help serve the customers after school. It gets a little rowdy when the workmen stop in for a beer or two, but there's more money in selling beer than ladies' pastry, Mr. Werner says. She hears all kinds of talk she'd rather not hear because she blushes easily, Ginna does, but she has to do it.

Her mouth is tight when she gets through waiting on tables, as if she bit off something hard. I don't like that funny new look on Ginna's face.

My other friend is Lara. She's the prettiest of the three of us. She's so pretty it makes me mad, but there are such amazing thoughts stirring in her head I forget about her being pretty. Being with Lara is like running outdoors after being cooped up inside; everything out there is blowing fresh and exciting.

Her eyes turn dark blue when she talks of the poor of the world, when she speaks of justice and a change for the better at long last, when she speaks of ideas. When she talks like that I can't sit still. I jump up and rearrange the chairs in the room, and plan a changed, better world along with Lara.

The front of her house is a small grocery store with big bulging sacks of potatoes by the door, and open vats of herring and pickles toward the back. Bread and salami sit on the counter ready to be cut, and blue onions and sausage and cheese dangle from iron hooks above it.

I love it at Lara's, with the hot smells of sausage and pickles and cheese that drive me wild with hunger, but Lara's ashamed of her home, I think. She always comes to mine to do her homework. It's quiet in my house, and everything's in its proper place. It's livelier at Lara's, where her little brothers stumble around spilling stuff by her mother's skirt while she cuts salami for customers, and wipes their noses and screams at them, too.

The Hellers are poor. Kaarl Heller spends his days running the store and playing chess and arguing politics, and what time is left at being a tailor. Bolts and bits of fabric are piled up all over waiting to be cut and sewn. But it's late in the afternoon when Mr. Heller's sewing machine begins to hum. It hums and sputters over the whines of René and Mischa and little Janneke then, over the customers' complaints, over supper, racing to make up for lost time.

Lara looks like her father. The same deep-blue eyes under thick lashes, the same jet-black hair, the same fair skin. But she's not grumpy and worn out the way he is, she's never tired. She's the best swimmer in school besides being the prettiest girl in class. And if you think that's unfair wait till you hear this.

We had a poll in class about who was the best-looking in eighth grade. We did it by points for hair and eyes and nose and developed bust, and even that Lara won. We were jealous. I was, anyway, but we all agreed Lara was *it;* it was scientific now.

But here's the funny thing. She doesn't seem to care that she's beautiful. It's natural to her, like breathing. Me with my flat chest and limp yellowish hair, I'd give anything to look like Lara, but Lara, all she thinks about is how to make the world a better place to live in.

Sometimes I wonder if Lara means she'd like to make her own home a better place to live in, but I cannot tell her that when she speaks of *injustice,* her eyes burning blue.

Sometimes skinny me feels it's just plain unjust I can't be as beautiful as my friend Lara. But I cannot tell her that, either.

Antwerp, November 17, 1939

Summers in New York are hot, so very hot that eggs are fried on city streets between shoot-outs. Gangsters roam the cities, and cowboys and Indians fire from the hip on galloping horses. I saw it in the cinema, so it must be true. It looks exciting, but I don't want to go there at all.

I don't want to go but just the same my feet know the way to the American consulate. I'm standing in front of it, application papers in hand.

Many people wait in a line that snakes halfway down

the tree-lined avenue. But here's another queue, this one very short.

"Why are some here and others there?" I ask a man in the long queue.

"The long queue is for those of us with lots of time," he explains. "Take me: I have to wait two years for my entrance visa, but everybody knows Poles have lots of time!" He laughs.

What is he laughing about? He wipes the sweat off his forehead and neck. Why is he perspiring on a cold November day?

"Psah! What's two years?" cries another man. "I have a ten-year wait. Ten years!" He spits in disgust.

"For a Rumanian ten years isn't bad," someone in the rear quips.

This is even funnier, it seems. Everyone is breaking up with laughter now.

"And you, little one, how long is your wait?"

I am bewildered. "I don't know," I say.

"But it's simple, child. Where were you born?"

"Here in Antwerp is where I was born!"

"In Belgium? You're a West European then? You belong with them there." He points to the short line and turns his back.

Rumanians, Poles, Greeks, Austrians, all East and South Europeans whose entry quota to America is limited huddle together. Seeking help, not finding it, they crack sad jokes to warm them.

Before the day is over I'm led upstairs to the medical examiner's.

"Your health's fine. Your IQ too. Congratulations, you've passed."

"What is IQ?" I ask.

"Intelligence quotient. You've passed just fine," the doctor says in his awkward French. "Now you must learn English. Ever belong to a party planning to overthrow the government?"

"Like the Flemish Nazis? Of course not!" The very idea makes me boil, but the doctor looks at his watch now.

"No," I answer quickly.

"Good girl. Welcome to the USA."

I hurry past the envious glance of the Polish man meeting me on the way out. The Rumanian is there too, still in the same place. He looks right past me, as if he has never seen me before.

The long queue is as long as before. Small wonder, too. The door marked ALL OTHERS at the top of the stairs is shut for the night, the blinds drawn tight over its mean little window.

I'm beginning to see why Maman says I'm lucky.

Antwerp, November 19, 1939

"Cleaning-out-drawers time," Maman says. "Throwing away stuff you don't need, like political pamphlets." She's still angry about it, Maman is, I can tell.

Well, here goes. "Oil for the Lamps of China," "The Coming War and Its Causes," "Lights Out in Spain," all in the trash basket.

There was a time—just last spring it was—when I

joined a Socialist group. These Socialists did not want to throw any government over at all, what they wanted was to throw a ball around. In the country preferably, on Sundays.

My friend Lara put me up to it. "Come along on a picnic," she said. "It's something to do on a Sunday, and besides, there are boys there too."

Knapsacks strapped to our backs, we rode our bikes to the potato fields just outside of Antwerp. All the potato plants were in flower and the countryside smelled strong and sweet at the same time. We sang songs about the Spanish Civil War. Something important was happening out there in the world. The people of Spain were losing the war and that was bad, but hearing about it from people who cared made me feel good. It made me feel part of that big world.

We played soccer then, and lunched on crusty bread and cheese. The grass was soft and dewy moist. It smelled fresh and the sky was new. We sang some more, and afterward there was a talk on the roots of war, and how it all came from the exploitation of the working class.

Charles led the discussions, mostly. Charles is sixteen and he'll be an engineering student at the Institut Polytechnique next year. He's good-looking in a freckled carrot-head kind of way, but best of all he's a baker's son. A true member of the proletariat, a laborer's son.

Even though Papa's an employer, Charles likes me, I think. He taught me steps in folk dancing and he always made room next to him when we sat in a circle singing. Sometimes he even put his arm around my shoulder.

And so I learned a lot at these Sunday picnics. I went straight home to tell Maman we had no right to live off the sweat of Papa's workers. There are two in his diamond-cutting shop. One saws or cleaves the rough diamond, the other shapes and polishes it. Both together don't labor the long hours Papa does—he decides how to work the diamond for its highest brilliance, and he does the buying and selling besides—but still they work *for* him. That must be exploitation, I think, and exploitation is bad.

"We must distribute our wealth," I told Maman. "All of it."

Maman blinked. "What wealth, child?"

"Our family wealth, of course. Aren't we rich?"

"No, child, we're not rich."

"But Papa has two men working for him, doesn't that make him rich?" Tears were beginning to irritate my eyes.

"Not yet it hasn't," Maman said.

"But—but Papa earns more than they do?"

She nodded, Maman did. "Sometimes," she said, "and sometimes not."

"Well then," I cried triumphantly, "shouldn't we share it with them?"

"Go wash up for supper," she said.

I had not won Maman over, I saw. I'd have to go to many more picnics to convince her. I had a cause now. Besides, I liked playing in the green potato fields, and best of all I liked being with boys.

Of course, we never see boys during the school week,

because their school is far from ours. I used to be shy with boys but now that I was a Socialist on Sundays I wasn't shy any longer.

Naturally Papa and Maman thought I went to the country for the fresh air. They didn't know about boys and rousing Spanish Civil War songs, but Lara says you're a true teenager only when you don't tell your parents everything anymore. She has many good ideas like that, Lara has.

Then one day Maman found out. Red hives sprouted over her arms and back from being so upset, and I had to promise not to be a Socialist ever again.

Antwerp, December 3, 1939

After Maman's hives there was no special place to go to on Sundays anymore. Lara still went to the Socialist picnics—Ginna had never gone to any, she is too shy—so now I just stayed home with her.

We still went to the park and played jump rope, or went rowing in the park's pond, or fed peanuts to the animals in the zoo, or rode our bikes to the port to munch French fries out of newspaper cones as we watched the ships come and go, but we'd always done that.

Then one day I found it, that special something. I joined Le Club de Mickey Mouse. It was not as grand as chanting "Workers of the world unite: You have nothing to lose but your chains," but it was special nonetheless.

Sponsored by the *Vlaamsche Gazette*, Antwerp's

Flemish newspaper, the Mickey Mouse correspondence service let you make friends all over the world. It was better than dreaming of faraway places. It was almost like sailing off on one of those ocean liners we were forever hanging about and really meeting new people.

My best pen pal was Ramon Oliveira from Nazaré, Portugal. He wrote about his father's fishing boat with its pointed prow and the fresh red trim of its sky-blue hull, and he wrote of sardine fishnets so large they covered his entire beach. I wrote about our purple-faced principal and told him how the Walloons had forced French on Flemish-speaking Antwerp, and I told him of Mme. Pinot's louse-hunting expeditions through our hair, too. And then he wrote about Nazaré's green ocean and bright flowers and I wrote about Antwerp's old burgher houses with their ladderlike roofs under the rainy skies.

Our letters wore our countries' prettiest stamps and then one day his photo arrived in the mail. He looked strong and dangerous the way his eyebrows knifed together, and he looked older than sixteen, but I sent him my picture anyway, the one where my pigtails shine very bright. And then a few weeks ago a letter came saying he was traveling north with his father and stopping in Antwerp for a visit.

If Maman got red hives from my Sunday Socialist picnics she was sure to get worse if Ramon from Portugal came to see me. Something had to be done.

"On Monday I'm being sent to a convent to spend the rest of my days in prayers and fasting," I wrote him then. "Adieu in this life forever, *mon très cher* Ramon,"

I added, and sprinkled drops of water on the letter to make it look like tears.

Today there was a letter from Portugal addressed to my parents.

I implore you to reconsider your cruel decision about your daughter's future. To be locked away in a convent at such a tender age is a fate worse than being buried alive. I beg you, indeed I beseech you, not to do this to your one and only daughter!

Please accept my most humble greetings.

Respectfully,
Ramon Oliveira

At the bottom of the letter it said, "P.S. My older sister suffered this fate and, alas, hanged herself in desperation."

Luckily Maman and Papa never saw the letter. I snatched it from the postman before it could reach them.

Antwerp, December 15, 1939

My official papers are set, my steamship ticket paid for, but Papa and Maman have nothing yet. The waiting time for their entry to America is too long, and Argentina and Colombia and Venezuela have flatly said no. They all want rich immigrants who can set up new businesses in their countries, not plain immigrants like my parents.

It looks like I'm leaving all by myself, and I've never been more miserable. If I'm lucky, what's it like to be unlucky?

Besides all that I just got my period. Suddenly there

was blood on my things and I was doubled over with cramps. All that bleeding was proof I was very sick for sure. But how could I tell Maman with so much on her mind already?

I broke down and sobbed. Maman found out and lifted me up in the air and cried, "Good luck, my poupeke, you're a young lady now!" She was beaming all over her face, and so what I thought a bad thing was really very good, it turned out, even if I was still afraid of all that blood coming out of me.

Now we boil the padded cotton strips I use in a great big pot and rinse them in clear water before hanging them up to dry in our backyard—three on one clothespin. There were those special times when I was shut out before, but now I'm part of it when that big pot boils and the kitchen steams up and smells of low tide. I'm the same as Maman now, full of hidden secrets as she is.

Antwerp, December 20, 1939

The sailing date on my ticket reads January 26, 1940, just a little more than a month away! And I still don't speak any English! We study it in school, of course, along with Latin and Greek and German as required foreign languages, but all I know are some stiff, stilted phrases.

My English tutor makes me feel even stiffer about it. Two afternoons a week he waits for me in our formal front parlor. "Have you done your lessons, Mademoiselle?" he asks.

"Oui, Monsieur . . . I mean, Yes, sir."

Antwerp, January 1, 1940

"So you're going to America, so big deal," Lara says to me today. "*Ça va*, it's all right of course, but me I'd rather be where things are happening."

"Leave her alone. She feels bad enough as it is!" cries Ginna.

We're on our way back from the docks where we've spent the day despite the steady drizzle. We're used to rain; it never bothers us, it's our climate. We watched coal from the south of Belgium loaded onto outbound freighters, and then we saw crates of oranges from Spain and figs and olives from Morocco taken off for us, and then the wind blew up mean. We rode our bicycles to a cheap mussels-and-French-fries restaurant, where it smelled hot and greasy, to warm up.

The place was jammed full. Everybody in Antwerp celebrates the holidays by feasting on mussels and beer, and Charles was there too.

As soon as he spotted us he picked up his beer and came over.

"A happy New Year!" he said, lifting his mug in the air. He said it to the three of us, but I felt he meant me and suddenly my face was beet red. Maybe he won't notice, I prayed, looking hard the other way.

No such luck, he's talking to me. "You're really leaving us, are you, Elke? And leaving us boys here to pine after you?"

Charles is teasing, I know, but my cheeks are so flushed I want to crawl under the floorboards to hide.

He winks at me, Charles does. "We'll just have to

write then, eh?" He laughs, and goes back to his friends. *"Au revoir, tot ziens, auf wiedersehen,* or how you say in English, so long!"

Ginna hadn't opened her mouth, but now she's bubbling over. "Do you really really think he'll write? Do you, do you?"

Does Ginna have a crush on Charles too? "I have a feeling he will," I say, "but only a feeling." My hands have stopped sweating.

"Girls can always tell when a boy likes them," Lara says with authority.

Lara is always sure of what she says, of course. But she's also Charles's first cousin, so maybe she really knows?

Antwerp, January 7, 1940

Maman rushes to consulates and other business but returns to prepare the midday meal, the main one of the day. Not long afterward she hurries out again, this time to come home laden with a crusty round Flemish bread and fruit in one arm and bundles of fresh cheese and herring in the other. This is for supper, the light evening meal.

Only now does the baking begin.

"Go down to the cellar and bring up the eggs and butter."

"But, Maman," I cry, seeing her drawn face.

"There *has* to be fresh pastry for supper," she snaps.

"But—but—let me go shop for it so you don't have to bake?"

Nothing's the same as before, yet Maman acts as if it is. There was never any reason to hound consuls before, yet that's what matters most now. It is the *only* thing that matters, but Maman still tries to keep things nice and first rate and orderly the way they used to be, even if it's all changed now.

"Hurry up, child, I haven't got all day. Get me the eggs and butter."

"But—but—"

"It has to be homemade to taste like anything, you know that. Papa wouldn't touch any of that store-bought stuff!"

So she's busy, Maman is, very busy. There is the little dressmaker to go to.

"American ready-to-wear simply doesn't compare in quality to the custom work here. No no, my daughter must have the best."

"But I don't care about clothes!"

"That's because you're such a tomboy now, always climbing trees and getting holes in everything, but how would it look to Tante Elise if my one-and-only's wardrobe wasn't up to date? What would she think? She'd think we don't care about you, that's what she'd think. Shush, child." Her fingers are on my lips. "Shush. You'll have the finest."

Maman's eyes are pulled back into her head.

"But of course I'm not tired," she cries impatiently. "Some things on my mind, that's all."

"Can I help, please, Maman, please?"

"You're too young."

Seeing my face sag, she giggles suddenly, that marvelous high-pitched giggle we so rarely hear around the house anymore.

"But after all, youth is a mistake that age corrects, isn't it?" She laughs, and for a fleeting moment I glimpse the spirited girl with the apple-red cheeks she must have been once, way back then.

"No, let me do it while I still can, child," she says then, serious again, her busy capable hands kneading, hemming, doing doing doing.

I wish I had a sister to talk to. I tell Ginna about Maman's pampering me.

"Maman's smothering me to death," I tell her. Right away I feel bad, having said something not nice about Maman to Ginna. Even if Ginna's my best friend in the whole world, it's not the same as saying something like that to a sister.

And there's something else too, something I haven't told anybody. There are times I'm afraid there's a fever in Maman now. She moves so fast, her eyes hot, the cheeks flushed purple in her white face.

Antwerp, January 23, 1940

Last day of school today, my last adieux. Mme. Hachette, the Latin teacher, kissed me on both cheeks and wished me *"Bonne chance en Amérique!"* And there were tears in back of Mevrouw Van Ruysbroeck's glasses as she warned me never to forget our precious Flemish literature. Or painting. "Remember our Breughel, our Rubens, our Van Eyck, our Memling," she cried, dabbing her eyes. Other nice things like that kept happening and something I thought I'd never feel happened: I felt sorry to leave L'Athénée Royale pour Jeunes Filles.

Ginna and I stroll along our waterfront. We skirt the busy jumble of docks and cranes and seamen as we go, not seeing any of it today. Ginna is my oldest friend and my very best friend, too. Our mothers walked us side by side in our baby carriages in the park and we've been close friends ever since.

I like Lara very much, also. We have such marvelous times together and she's such an original, Lara is. But Ginna, Ginna I love more than anyone.

The inseparables, we're called, or *double Pat-et-Patachon,* after our favorite comic-strip characters, because Ginna's short and fat, like Pat, and I'm long and skinny, like Patachon.

Unlike glum Pat-et-Patachon we laugh a lot. We laugh all the time. Anything sets us off into gales of laughter. Purple grapes bobbing on our librarian's Sunday hat, a boy on a bike cross-eyed with shyness as he smiles at us, a laborer clomping clumsy and loud in his wood sabots, anything at all.

But today we don't laugh, we don't even talk as we walk, each in her own little hole of misery. Ginna hates my leaving her; I hate to go.

On and on we walk, our steps on the cobbles the only sound. The brooding skies loom low and turn dark. It is raining. Some schoolboys splatter us as they run past, shouting, *"Jood, Jood, Krist 'hedd'e gy vermoord!"* "Jew, Jew, Christ killer!" I look at Ginna staring straight ahead as if she had not heard, and I'm afraid for her suddenly.

We walk on in silence, the streetlights like shimmering yellow moons on the wet streets now. It is raining, raining, a true Low Country rain, dreary, endless, yet soft.

After a time we hum an old favorite, Ginna and I:

> *Il pleut sur la route*
> *Dans mon coeur j'écoute*
> *Le bruit de tes pas.* . . .

> Rain falls on the road
> In my heart I listen
> To the sound of your steps. . . .

as the wetness slowly seeps through us.

"We're all coming to the boat," Ginna says then. "Me and Lara of course, and Denise and Mathilde and Anna; most of the kids from school are coming. Did I forget Charles? Charles has the flu, but he is leaving his sickbed for you. *Seulement pour toi.*" She laughs. "For you alone."

Ginna feels sorry for me, I think. She makes up stories to make me feel better about leaving home—she's such a friend. I'll never have a real friend like that again. Never.

Charles—Charles likes me then? It's as if Ginna hears my thoughts. "Of course Charles likes you. Didn't he give you a photo album with a beautiful design around a poem he made up special?" The poem is a going-away gift inside another gift, which is an album filled with pictures of all my friends.

I blush scarlet just thinking of it, and punch Ginna in the ribs with my elbow, Antwerp fashion, and suddenly we're laughing again, laughing till our cheeks are wet from laughing and crying both.

Antwerp, January 25, 1940

The day has come. There are no more errands to do, no more cousins once removed to visit. It's all done, there's nothing more to do.

I take the trolley one last time. It clanks along past the ancient Flemish burgher houses with their stepped roofs like ladders reaching up to the skies, past our own Flemish Rubens's mansion, past the dazzling flower market behind the blackened ancient cathedral, on toward the noisy, busy fish stalls.

What if I jumped off and hid here among the fishmongers? They'd never find me, never, never. I could earn my keep scrubbing mussels, frying French fries and wrapping them, all hot and crisp and delicious, in newspaper cones to sell. . . .

The trolley rattles on. It rattles past that tangled jumble of wharves and docks that is our bustling port, and then turns back.

Those sights, I want to rivet them into my head, to fasten them there forever. But even as I cling to them I begin to feel them peeling away from me. The sights are turning into memories that drift off into the past like petals in a light breeze.

Only Antwerp's wet smell of mussels and fish lingers on.

My ship, the *Volendam*, lies in the river Schelde, waiting to swallow me up.

Papa and Maman are here on the pier with me. Ginna is here, too, of course, and Lara and Charles, and Gisèle and Denise and Anna and Mathilde and Minna. Even Frans came, and Frans never sees anyone since he came back from the war in Spain with that limp.

Boxes are being carried up the ramp, crates are being hoisted up, all sorts of people are scurrying about the *Volendam*. There is much coming and going, much confusion and noise, but within me it is silent.

"That man, I know him!" Papa lurches forward to snatch the man's hand. "Mr. Muller, will you keep an eye on my daughter here during the crossing? Will you please?" There's a funny look on my father's face I never saw before.

"Sure," Mr. Muller, a casual business acquaintance, says. "Sure, why not?"

"Sure," Mrs. Muller says, nodding and smiling. She takes her child's hand tightly in hers and moves on.

My right hand grips my left hard as my friends crowd around me.

"Write often, eh?"

"Sure, I'll write. I'll write often."

"Don't go sending us letters in English, eh?"

"That crazy language that twists your mouth all over your face? Not a chance!" For the first time I'm laughing.

"Don't forget your Flemish," cries Minna. "Or your French," cries Denise.

"Don't forget me!" "Or me!!"

No matter what, don't forget us.

I won't forget, I won't forget ever—but will you not forget me?

"Remember," I hear Maman through the thick fog of fear that is fast enveloping me, "remember, here's your key." She knots the key about my neck like an amulet. "Any time you want to come back you've got the key," she jokes, smiling through her wet face. There's a little cry, quickly stifled, as she chucks me under the chin.

"Simple," Papa says.

"Very simple," we all say, knowing it's not, laughing at ourselves for making believe it's simple.

"Couldn't be simpler," we agree, crying at the finality of the last farewell.

Tears are rolling down our faces from trying so hard to laugh.

The ship's horns sound their second warning.

"You must go now," Papa says gently, very gently.

I really must go. Why, I forget just now.

A last embrace, and I'm running up the gangplank into the *Volendam*.

I did not remember Maman's cheek was so very soft.

Antwerp, January 26, 1940
At night

They were all standing on the pier waving to me here on deck of the *Volendam*. They seemed to be going off to the side then. But no, it was me moving, my ship that was pushing away from shore.

"Elleke, Elleke," I heard, I thought I heard faintly through the loud blasting of the ship's horns. Maman was calling me still.

But Maman had sliced herself off from me. She was blurring, they were all blurring now. Papa, Maman, Ginna, Lara, Charles, Frans, and the others, melting away in the grayness of Antwerp's skies.

Only the foghorns were calling now.

On ship, January 27, 1940

All night long the foghorns called to me in my mother's voice as I tossed about on my narrow bunk.

At daybreak two young ladies stagger into the cabin. They are tipsy and loud. On the bunk below me a middle-aged woman sobs into her pillow to muffle the sound of her weeping. She mumbles something in German. The words are close to Flemish but not quite.

I don't know what to do. I give her my last dry handkerchief. She stuffs her whole face into it. "My husband is gone," she sobs. "I'm alone, all alone."

Her crying makes me weep harder too, but not so much for her as for me.

In the other bunks the two drunk girls are still giggling.

It's late in the morning when I peek out of my porthole. After a long night of listening to the ship's throb and gurgle all is strangely still.

We've reached the mouth of the English Channel, but the *Volendam*'s motors have stopped churning. My heart pounds with wild hope suddenly and I'm up on deck in minutes. Mr. Muller is there peering through his binoculars.

"Why aren't we moving?" I ask him. "Are we turning back? Are we?"

Maybe it's all been a monstrous mistake and we're on our way back to Antwerp?

The mad hope doesn't last.

"See that shipwreck?" Mr. Muller says, pointing toward the left of the bow on the open sea. "That boat sinking over there?" I see a skeleton of a ship drifting in the waters through Mr. Muller's binoculars, and I see waves washing over its hull. "That passenger boat exploded on a mine!" he cries. "The seas are full of mines, there are German submarines all over! You can't see them," he shouts, "but the war is raging in these waters all about us!"

Mr. Muller's eyes are wild. Mr. Muller is frightened. Could a grown-up like Mr. Muller be more afraid than I am?

"Are we going to be hit next?" I scream, panicked. "Are we?"

All eyes are on the empty rowboats coming back from the wrecked ship now. There are no survivors, the crewmen report. Only bodies floating in the water. It is too late to help them. What can we do? An SOS has been radioed. What else is there?

We're bunched together in knots taking turns at the lonely pair of binoculars. The gutted ship lists more than before. We pace the decks, watching it go down.

Only the very top of the smokestacks can be seen anymore. The last one has gone under now, sunk below the waves. The ship is gone, buried at sea. And I never even saw a funeral before. "What if we bump into a torpedo and burst into burning bits?" I ask a girl my age called Monique, hanging on to her. "Do we just drown then, the way they did, just like that, here in this cold sea?"

On ship, January 29, 1940

I'm not as alone as I thought I was. The Meyers and the Seftons are as bewildered as I am, and so are the Strausses. Monique is tearful about those she left behind, just as I am, and we talk about it all the time, she and I. And Ilga from Leipzig and Yvette from Nice and Dori from Vienna are filled with dread for what's ahead. I'm not the only one who's afraid.

Her speed cut down, the *Volendam* propels herself cautiously, carefully picking her way among the mines. We are coming out of the English Channel into the rough open waters of the Atlantic Ocean now.

Howling winds greet us as we come around the bend. Suddenly our ship lurches forward and pitches. We are bobbing up and down now, the black waves boiling and foaming as they crash against our side.

The *Volendam* is a small ship, and there is not enough ballast in her hold to keep her steady in a North Atlantic storm. She does not carry much freight and there are too few steamer trunks aboard to balance the load properly. Most of the German and Austrian passengers aboard fled the Nazis in too great a hurry to pack a trunk, and feel lucky just to have gotten their entry papers before the American quotas filled up. Half full, our little *Volendam* tosses and totters crazily in the angry seas.

My stomach is up high by my throat and threatens to go higher. I'm not thinking about Papa and Maman and feeling lonely. I'm not thinking about the panic of fleeing penniless from brutality and terror. I've even forgotten about undersea mine explosions. I'm too sick to care.

High winds whistle across blustery skies and churn the seas up more. Ship's stewards skate across the slippery decks carrying cardboard boxes to vomit into, but everywhere green-faced people are doubled over the rail retching miserably. I stretch out flat to steady myself but the horizon tilts wildly and comes right at me. It's all I can do to keep my soup down.

On ship, February 1, 1940

I woke to a sunny day this morning, a beautiful day. The skies are clear and the sea sparkles. Everyone is smiling. A man walks up to me and puts his arm about my shoulders. "Just a little kiss for being alive," he says, pushing his face up close. His unshaven cheeks are blue and rough. He's old, he must be twenty for sure. I draw back. "You'll regret saying no all your life, sweetheart," he says.

I don't care, I like Ulli Meyer better. Ulli is from Berlin and Monique's from Paris and I'm from Antwerp, but we're friends already.

On ship, February 10, 1940

Nothing but green and blue shimmering about, and deep purple beyond. Ocean and sky are one; it's all there is. Where we were is water, where we're heading is water, water as far as I can see, way into tomorrow. The sea is my mother, she envelops me.

The days stretch on and on. Is it fourteen, fifteen days now? The Muller family Papa spoke to at Antwerp's dock says, "How are you?" when we meet and I say, "*Bien, merci*, and you?" and we walk on. I turned thirteen somewhere along the way and Monique sang Happy Birthday to me in French and Ulli in German and suddenly I missed Maman and Papa so much I broke into sobs.

We've been at sea so long I've lost track; I cannot even remember the feel of solid ground underfoot. We play shuffleboard and huddle around Ulli and his recorder, singing folksongs for hours on end and I try to forget the bad things. I rarely cry anymore, and then only in my cabin at night. The two girls are in the bar, as usual, and my middle-aged bunkmate is out playing gin rummy. I'm alone, and can cry all I want. My mother the sea rocks me then, rocks me till I fall asleep.

. . . Thick towels warmed our shivering bodies when we came out of the icy North Sea. We rolled in the soft white sand and built castles topped with tottering turrets of trickled mud. . . . "Elleke, we're going home!" Maman's high voice is calling me. "You're cold, child, you're blue with cold!" She wraps the terry tight about me. The towel feels scratchy, warm.

My dream is warm.

We're moving closer to the other side where America lies. America! I picture it bright yellow like the map, the red dots of Chicago, Boston, Detroit, New York, Seattle, going round and round it, round and round, until I'm dizzy.

On ship, New York, February 12, 1940

And now it's seventeen days since we sailed and New York's skyline slides out of the clouds to greet us. It looms high and dark, as unreal as a stage set. Slowly the giant skyscrapers shift into focus, stone on stone on still more stone.

We crowd up on deck, all of us. "New York, it's really New York!" As we come closer some of my friends begin to sing. The Seftons are the loudest; they're shouting with joy and relief at finally being here. The Meyers and the Strausses are singing softly, so softly it seems more like praying.

Suddenly Monique yells, "The shore, I can almost touch it!" her voice high, high above the singing. It's the real thing then, it's really real! We laugh and cry and hug each other, and then turn quiet, totally quiet as we sink into ourselves and our own thoughts.

What if no one comes to meet me here in this strange country? What if Uncle Jacques forgot?

But we've not really landed yet, it seems, we've only docked temporarily at Ellis Island for our papers to be searched. Immigration officials swarm on board. Big lumbering Gary Cooper types, casually, comfortably chewing gum as they ask us questions. Everything will be all right.

But what is this? The Meyer family with their two sons are summoned aside to follow them off the boat to Ellis Island. Ulli Meyer, my friend, throws me a strange look as he leaves with the officers, a look that says, Is it starting all over again—the harassment we thought we left behind?

"What's wrong? What could it be?" I cry to Mr. Sefton. After all the terrible things that happened to them in Berlin this isn't right, this singling out for more questioning. It should have been easier for them now.

"Perhaps their papers aren't in order," he shrugs. "Or, who knows, some sickness has been reported."

I remember Frau Meyer's coughing fits, and I fear for them.

And Maman and Papa, and all my friends back home, I think suddenly. What lies ahead for them?

February 13, 1940
AMERICA!

We've landed in Hoboken, USA. We're in the vast vaulted hall that serves as port of entry for the welcome newcomers to America. Solid land feels wobbly under my sea legs, and my head is dizzy from all the busy doings around here.

I've gone past the friendly immigration officers who have stamped my papers and said, "Welcome to the USA," with big smiles, past the not-so-friendly customs men rummaging through my baggage for smuggled

Refugee

goods and dirty French books, past the kind social
worker who so wants to help.

"No English," I tell her. "No speak English."

She is annoyed. "No English at all?"

I shake my head. I've forgotten all the English Mr.
Tuttle taught me these past few months. His smoke-
stained fingertips impatiently tapping the table flash back
at me, but no English.

A familiar face materializes, grinning warmly. Uncle
Jacques pats me on the head. "And the pigtails, little one,
what happened to the pigtails? But you're not the pesty
tomboy I remember at all, why you're all grown up,
a veritable young lady now!"

"Uncle Jacques! Uncle Jacques!" I throw myself at
him and we hug tight. The last time I saw him he was
passing through from his native Vienna on his way to
America. His bride Elise was with him, but all I remember of her is lots of red hair like a flame and dangling
earrings. I was eleven then.

"The family, how are they?" Uncle Jacques is speaking kindly but rapidly, asking many questions, now in
French, now in German.

"I don't remember."

"Papa's blood pressure they wrote me about, is it still
so high?"

"I forget."

Jacques looks at me. "And Maman, how is she?"

"I don't know."

I don't know anything. I wish my boat had sunk and
I'd gone down with it. It would've been better than

]49[

standing around tongue-tied in America; anything would've been better. Uncle Jacques sprang out of New York's stony skyline to rescue me, but I'm dazed and dumb, a real dummy. He wants news from home, but I have no news. Suddenly I remember nothing, nothing at all.

Alien sounds confuse me. Strange faces crowd in on me, frighten me. If I'd gone down with the boat everything would be all over. If only I had.

Jacques looks at me oddly. "*Ça va*, little one? Are you all right?"

"*Ça va*, I'm all right," I lie.

"This room will be your home," Tante Elise says later, showing me the cubicle behind the kitchen in their apartment. The tiny room has a tinier window that faces a brick wall with an eye-sized window an arm's length away.

"*Merci*, Tante Elise. It's lovely," I lie.

I hate the small room with no view. I hate my tiny window facing the other tiny window that looks at me. I hate the dark little bedroom behind the cluttered kitchen in the overcrowded apartment. I hate the dark narrow building the apartment sits in. I hate the buildings streaked with soot and black rain that line our gloomy street, I hate it all!

Later that night I stifle my sobs as I bite the skimpy pillow, missing the ample one I left back home. I miss my own room, my own big brass bed in the middle, the family's rolltop desk on one end, the heavy wardrobe with the creaky mirrored door next to it. When Marieke the cat wasn't curled up on my billowing goosefeather comforter she liked to take flying leaps onto the desk, scattering papers all over the room, my own wonderful room with the plump pink and red roses spattered all over its walls and ceiling, I miss it, I miss it. I miss Maman, I miss Papa, I miss my friends, I'm so miserable I want to die.

New York, February 16, 1940

My first day of school in America today, and it was something. I mean it was awful. Mrs. Harris, the principal, talked to me for a time but I did not understand most of what she said. She was smiling though, Mrs. Harris was, and this on a plain Tuesday morning. Our principal, Mme. Pinot, only smiles at Christmas and Easter, and even then mostly when parents come with gifts for teachers, and vacation time is ahead.

Anyway there was smiling Mrs. Harris bringing me to my homeroom and telling the class, "Here is Elke Colbert, just arrived from Antwerp, Belgium, and we're all going to welcome her to America, aren't we?"

My knees were knocking so loud I had trouble hearing what else she said. I had trouble standing up, in fact. I stared down at my feet to force them to keep quiet and then I looked at the students and saw they were laughing, and I was sure they were laughing at me for my loud knees.

It seemed like it was never going to end, this standing up in front of the class in my mustard-colored sweater and drab brown skirt, but then Mrs. Harris said something else and the students sat down. We went back to her office and she told me she liked the color of my sweater, and was it handmade, she wanted to know.

No principal in Belgium would ever talk like that to an ordinary student. Mrs. Harris must have wanted to make me feel better. She must have heard my knees knocking and felt sorry for me, that's why she said nice things about my sweater. And she did make me feel nice, except my stomach was all cramped up.

It's still hurting this afternoon after two glasses of tea with lemon. Tante Elise thought the tea would soothe me nicely. "It's only nerves, Elke," she said. "You're nervous, that's all. Tomorrow will be easier."

Tomorrow! My belly's curled up in knots just thinking about it. Maybe I'll be lucky and be too sick to go to school tomorrow?

New York, February 19, 1940

George Washington in upper Manhattan, my school in the new country, is a big drafty place jumping with noise. Boys and girls jostle each other and crash through the corridors laughing and screaming. Gum wrappers and cigarette butts litter the toilets where they dash in for a quick smoke. Everybody, but everybody, smokes between classes.

Nothing about school here is at all like L'Athénée Royale pour Jeunes Filles back home. Serious, obedient, devoted to books, we were forever clamped down and hushed, so clamped and cramped anything at all exploded us into wild giggling fits.

Here all is open, freshly scrubbed of the past, and free. Only the new matters here in the New World. Boys and girls together in classes feels like an ongoing party, not like school at all, and I like that a whole lot.

Nobody even looks like a student here. They don't wear uniforms the way we did, navy blue from top to bottom, with berets and long wool stockings till late July when school ended. They can wear what they like here.

The boys are rough and pimply like the boys in Antwerp, but they seem more grown-up. The girls' voices sound hard as metal, but they look so soft. Like long frail reeds they look in their pale baby-soft sweaters that cling tight. And everything about them shines. Their hair, their teeth, their freshly painted nails and lips, everything.

I slink through the corridors, a lusterless mouse. The muted browns and maroons and russets of my custom-made clothes look hopeless, so dim and drab next to the pinks and oranges and sharp greens the other girls wear. And my shoes, my fine hand-sewn leather shoes, how prim they look next to the shining bobby sox and saddle shoes!

I cling to the corridor walls, making myself as small as I can.

Antwerp, February 20, 1940

Elleke chérie!

There you are in faraway America! Do you see cowboys and Indians on horses? And real gangsters? Real live gangsters with blazing guns? What an exciting life you must have. Nothing exciting ever happens here. It's gray and rainy as usual, and everybody's talking about the war that's coming, as usual, but nothing is happening.

A lot of boys are in uniform now, and walking to school is more fun than it used to be because soldiers just love girls. But even the soldiers are bored standing around with nothing to do all day. If only something would happen!

Is there really gold in the streets of New York? Ha ha. Of course not, that's only a saying, Elleke, isn't it? Because if true you'd be sending some of it to your old friends, I'm sure. The price of things is sky-high, and climbing still. Papa is a bundle of nerves these days. So is Maman. Everybody's jumping at everybody's throat.

I ride my bike to the old port and watch the ocean liners come and go like the tide, and all good things still seem possible then.

> *Write, write!*
> *Your friend,*
> *Ginna*

New York, March 2, 1940

Dear Papa and Maman,

I haven't seen any cowboys or gangsters but it's very nice here in New York. Uncle Jacques and Tante Elise are very nice to me, they take me on the fast subways and to the quick food places they have here. We went to such a restaurant—the Automat it's called—and all you have to do is stick some coins into a slot and one of the sandwiches that's sitting on a shiny shelf behind glass pops right out! I think that's marvelous, don't you?

Now I'll tell you what a sandwich is. It's two slices of bread back to back with some chopped-up fish or meat or cheese in between, but it's not as disgusting as it sounds because we squeeze thick runny tomato stuff on it that covers up the taste!

I'm liking it a lot here in America as you can see, but I wish you'd hurry up and join me here, I wish,

I wish, I wish!

Kisses and hugs,
your Elleke

New York, March 3, 1940

Dear Ginna and Lara,

Yesterday I wrote a letter to Papa and Maman that was full of lies. I told them I loved it here in New York, but I really hate it. I said I was excited about the new foods here but the truth is they make me throw up, but I don't want them to worry about me so I said what I did. And I didn't want them to know that the subways scare me the way they rumble off fast into long, dark tunnels.

I'm so lonely, inside me is like a black tunnel.

Write, please write!
Elke

New York, March 10, 1940

New York's high stony streets are dizzying with swirling papers flying in the wind. Shreds of newsprint dance above our heads. My face down to keep from seeing the headlines, I run, but the frightful words rush at me as I run. BLACKOUT! the headlines scream. LIGHTS OUT OVER EUROPE!

What's it like over there now? I write home, but the letters I get are few. The answers in them tell very little. Everyone is either trying to leave or just waiting. Waiting for the invasion they say won't happen or waiting for orders. All is quiet but deep down they all know it's coming.

A letter from home came today!

Antwerp, March 1, 1940

Elleke mine,

So you like the life in America, eh? And your uncle and aunt are good to you, child? We knew they would be. They are good, decent people. If only we too could be with you!

Forgive me, but you seem farther away than ever now that it looks as if we cannot go anywhere. We're grateful you're safe and in good hands, and we're not giving up hope yet.

I kiss you and hug you,
Maman

P.S. Dear Elleke, You know your Maman has a pessimistic nature and worries too much. She's lucky to have an optimist like me for a husband, and I'm telling her and you that all we need is a little luck and money and we'll be on our way to Brazil!

Be strong!
Your ever-loving Papa

P.P.S. To show you I mean what I say: I'm making arrangements to have Cousin Josef and his family stay in our house when we leave.

Papa does not want me to worry, that's why he says hopeful things to me. But what if no country takes them in? What if they can't get out at all?

I hope Papa is right in being an optimist.

New York, March 16, 1940

Our Bavarian neighbor has adopted me. She lives in the apartment next door to ours here on West 182nd Street. Many people live in these tall buildings on our windy block. Old people with pets and young couples with children and tricycles and baby carriages, but no one speaks to anyone else.

Frau Braun is different from the others. She is fat and forty and she loves to talk and tell stories. Her eyes twinkle in her jolly face then, and everything about her comes alive. But her own story is not funny at all.

"They stormed in one day, those Nazis, out of the blue they came, and asked my Walter to come with them to sign some papers at City Hall. They were laughing and saying something about resettlement in the East, I remember, but they were laughing so much it did not sound serious to me, his following them in the car. *'Keine Sorge, gnädige Frau.* Do not worry, dear lady,' they told me, but I never saw my Walter again."

Frau Braun's eyes cloud up funny when she talks about her Walter, but she never cries. She's matter-of-fact, Frau Braun is, cool yet warm and cozy, and never sorry for herself. There are times when I've found her sitting alone in the dark, staring out at nothing, but she never never cries.

What she likes best is baking. She bakes coffee cakes and apple tarts for the people in the apartments on our floor. She bakes because it's someone's birthday, or it's snowing out, or the weekend's coming. She's always baking, and the sweet smell of cinnamon and yeast is like my mother's kitchen in winter.

I like Frau Braun, I really do.

Antwerp, March 10, 1940

Ma très chère Elke,

You will not think me too bold if I call you my very dear? I so wanted to call you that before, but didn't dare to, not before. You're not like other girls who giggle and blush all the time, you're deep. You listen. I knew you knew how I felt that day we rode our bikes home in the rain and didn't talk. Now you're gone and I miss you.

I'm going on military maneuvers next week. My parents are still pacifists. They claim it's nothing but more saber rattling, but me I'm glad to be doing something at last. This war of nerves is making me nervous!

Toujours moi,
Charles

P.S. I send you my photo so you won't forget me. How do you like me in uniform, eh?

New York, March 20, 1940

I gaze at Charles, handsome in his uniform. He's seven-teen, a man now.

"I like the rain in your hair," he said, touching it. It was two Sundays before I left. We had stopped at the corner of my street. A steady soft drizzle was coming down as we said good-bye. "Will I see you again?" he asked. We stood close, our bike handlebars clinking metal against metal in the wet.

"Somewhere," I said. "Who knows?"

"Who knows?" he said.

I tuck Charles's snapshot inside my blouse, where it is safe.

New York, March 25, 1940

I really like Frau Braun a lot. She likes me more than Tante Elise does. Tante Elise doesn't like me at all. Not what I say, not what I don't say. "Don't waste time reading French, you're in America now," she says, shut-ting my Colette book. "Go curl your hair instead; it's hanging there limp as boiled noodles."

Just looking at me makes Tante Elise sigh. She's nice enough, feeding me vitamins when I'm lonely and stuff, but just the same I'd rather be with Frau Braun, who likes me the way I am. Things have to be just so with Tante Elise: books upright, magazines stacked, drawers shut tight. Why, at times she reminds me of Mme. Pinot! Poor Uncle Jacques, he's too weary to see his wife as she really is. To him she's the best and most beautiful woman in the world.

The thirteen-year-old with the mousy straight hair stares back at me in the mirror. Yes, I'm jealous of Tante Elise. I make a face, stick my tongue out and slap her—ouch, that hurt. You're prettier when you smile, I tell her. Much. Don't frown, it makes your eyes small as slits.

I open them wide and put on a fierce expression. *Zut,* I can't look as dramatic as Tante Elise when she creates a scene no matter what I do. I bare one shoulder. I bare both shoulders for that devastating décolleté look of hers, but it doesn't work. I'm still bony and flat on top. My legs are good, much better than Tante Elise's piano-stool legs, but whoever looks at legs? Not Uncle Jacques, surely, not someone fine like Uncle Jacques.

It's hopeless, hopeless. Some of Tante Elise's cherry lipstick smeared on thick somehow makes my eyes shine in the mirror. How about some of her mascara, now, some of that luscious turquoise eyeshadow of hers? There now, for that femme-fatale look!

I should have let Ramon from Portugal rescue me when there was still time, I tell the dazzling creature in the mirror. I was the woman in his life, and I was cruel enough to tell him I'd be secluded in a convent for the rest of my days. How could I be so heartless? Ramon, no, Ramon wouldn't allow me to feel lost and lonely in New York, forever in Tante Elise's shadow. Never.

Ramon wasn't the only man in your life, there was Charles too, that girl in the mirror reminds me. And Raphael, remember Raphael? Of course, Raphy from Zurich. Him I met while on vacation with Maman's cousins the Lows in Switzerland, *the* high point of last summer.

Herta, the Lows' eighteen-year-old daughter, asked me to come along with her friends on an overnight hike, and was I flattered. All five thousand feet to the top of Mount Rigi to watch the sunrise we yodeled, the six of us hikers. We had been walking the entire night, a trudging, bone-crushing, exhilarating climb, and by the time we reached the top we simply crumpled in a heap. It was later, when we woke in the sun, that Raphael kissed me.

The tops of the trees lit up first, I remember. Their outline reddened as the sky went wide awake and sharp blue. The sun was there, a ripe tomato about to burst, bursting then, the icy lakes below glittering in the sunburst.

From fighting red the sun mellowed into warm caramel and melted into honey. We stretched under that melting sunshine, warm at last, and yawned and stretched some more, and slept. . . .

Quickly now: Tante Elise's makeup off, my face scrubbed clean, I slide under the covers to meet Raphael once more in my sleep. "Your hair is like honey," he whispers as he kisses me, "soft as melting honey." I am floating on a bed of delicious dreams.

"Hurry up in there, schooltime, schooltime!"

There is no Raphael anymore, there's only Tante Elise knocking on my bedroom door, her great green eyes flashing with annoyance at my laziness.

"Coming, Tante Elise!" I slam my dreams shut to face the raw March day in New York.

New York, April 9, 1940

REICH FORCES TAKE COPENHAGEN / BOMB OSLO IN
SUDDEN BLOW / NORWAY DECLARES WAR ON GERMANY

I'm stunned. Uncle Jacques's head is buried in the newspaper and Tante Elise's lips are thin wires drawn tight in her face as she busies herself about the apartment emptying ashtrays that'll soon be filled with burnt-out cigarettes. The radio is on, blaring out news bulletins, commentaries, opinions, more bulletins.

Today is Tuesday. Current Events Club day. At least there'll be kids to talk to after classes. Some of the school's brightest students are in this group; they know what's going on in the world. They care about the momentous stuff that's happening.

Jackie, who's number one in American history, opens the discussion. "What does today's invasion of Denmark and Norway mean to us here?" she asks.

"The war is spreading, obviously," Brian says. Brian is crazy about military tactics. "The Germans are on the offensive and are way ahead."

"Yes, of course; but what does it have to do with us?"

Keep calm, I tell myself.

"What Jackie wants to know is will there be more jobs in the U.S. if the war expands," Dick explains. Dick's father is a labor lawyer and Dick knows all about economics.

I'm taken aback at the coldheartedness. "But—but—" I stammer stupidly, "isn't America friends with the Scandinavian countries?"

"Sure we are. But we don't have to go to war to save them, do we? We're not our brother's keepers, are we?"

My knuckles are white; I've been gripping the table too hard. I leave, slamming the door behind me, and run home to turn the radio on. So much for extracurricular Current Events afternoons. No one cares, that's all.

Edward R. Murrow is reporting from London. His warm voice, calm but concerned, somehow connects me back to the world.

New York, April 10, 1940

I've been at school since my first week here, but I'm still not used to it, it feels so big and cold and indifferent. At least the school day is shorter than back home and I like that, I like that a whole lot. And I like having boys in class, even if I'm as shy as I used to be before those Sunday Socialist picnics in Antwerp.

School was never anything I was wild about, but back home I had friends and that made things possible. I don't have any friends here at George Washington school. I don't have any friends in this country at all.

When I speak English, and I have to, all the time, "the" sounds like "de" or sometimes "ze," and words with R in them gargle back in my throat instead of rolling up front and it all comes out funny and wrong, so I'd rather stick to what I know. At least I understand what I'm saying then.

Uncle Jacques handed me a dollar bill this morning. "Get small change," he said. "Practice your English." So I jumped up and ran to the corner drugstore. "Can you *wissel?*" I asked the big man behind the counter. "Oh, baby, can I whistle!" he laughed, and people turned around to look at me and laughed, and I grew red and fled. *Wissel* means exchange in Flemish, of course, but could it mean something like flirting in English?

That's why I miss the new friends I met on the boat so much. But Monique has moved to New Orleans where her father found a job selling insurance to French-speaking customers, so she's gone. I had a letter from Ulli with the good news that the whole Meyer family was allowed to stay in the U.S. It made me so happy to hear that. But later I felt angry that Maman and Papa don't have the same luck—immigration quotas are plain unfair! —and I didn't write back for a long time.

Anyway Ulli lives in Brooklyn, more than an hour by subway from Washington Heights in Manhattan where I am, and neither of us has a phone because we're poor, and that's too bad. It's hard to have a friend you don't see or talk to, so what I do is visit Frau Braun instead. Her butter cookies crumble soft and sweet in my mouth and I forget I'm scared about things happening over there, especially to those I care about back home in Antwerp.

New York, April 17, 1940

What's going on with Maman and Papa? It's been weeks since we heard from them, weeks and weeks.

They would have written before they left, if they did leave.

They would have, wouldn't they?

Their last letter was dated March first, but there has been no mail since. How discouraged they must feel, and sad, not being wanted in any country at all. A big buzzing world out there, and no room to give my parents refuge anywhere.

Uncle Jacques and I talk about it, but after a while there's nothing more to say and he goes back to studying his Plato, a sure sign he's worried sick.

Could they have given up? Trying to leave, I mean?

When I was still in Antwerp most people said Belgium would stay neutral. The same as Holland did in the Great War, and hadn't the Dutch been smart? Here in America everyone says the German invasion of Western Europe is around the corner, and that means Belgium, but over there they don't believe it can happen.

I am so worried.

Charles was the last one to write to me, and that was over a month ago. And my best friends, why haven't they written to me? War is coming, but where is everybody?

I am worried.

New York, April 19, 1940

April winds howl outside, but here in the apartment high up on the fifteenth floor it's warm and snug. Promptly at four in the afternoon Tante Elise plays Mah-Jongg with her friends.

Whipped cream waits in the fine china bowl, ready for the strong black coffee and rich Viennese pastries. Cups clatter, ladies chatter, perfume mingles with cigarette smoke: The cozy time is here. Dimples appear on Tante Elise's cheeks now that she smiles, and Tante Elise always smiles at this hour.

Before the game she has worked six hours embroidering sequins on evening purses. Piecework, it's called. Squinty hard work is what it is, and squinty is what she is when she rises round-shouldered from the long hours of work, squinty and mean. But now that it's Kaffeeklatsch time she's all pink and soft and lovable.

Uncle Jacques is a hardworking watchmaker here, nothing like the promising young lawyer she married back in Vienna's carefree days, and the money he earns does not go far. He's irritable these days, sharp with short snappy words that lash and hurt his wife's feelings. Tante Elise weeps easily, and worry creases are beginning to show in Uncle Jacques's handsome face.

They haven't been here long. They came right after the *Anschluss* when Hitler annexed Austria two years ago, and they still don't speak English well. To practice law Uncle Jacques would have to go to law school and pass the American bar exams, and there's neither money nor time for that. About all he and Tante Elise can manage is to go to the night school for foreigners and study English.

"*Wien, Wien, nur du allein* . . ." Vienna, only you, Vienna, will forever be the city of my dreams . . . she hums. Who knows, if Tante Elise had stayed in Vienna and Vienna had remained carefree, if there had been no Hitler and no *Anschluss*, perhaps she would be different. Who knows, she might be as mellow as the late afternoons she so loves.

"*Wien, Wien, nur du allein . . .*" she sings, that nostalgic song of old Vienna, her favorite. She is beautiful now, her flaming hair framing a face that is calm and soft. I love Tante Elise when she sings.

New York, April 20, 1940

A letter from Antwerp came in the mail today, but not from my parents. It was from my friend Lara, but it did not make me feel very good.

Here's what it said:

Antwerp, April 10, 1940

Elke!

Trouble is on the way. I feel it in my bones. We're buying all the flour and sugar and oil we can buy, but the prices are so high we can only buy a little bit of this and a little bit of that.

The streets are filled with Flemish Nazis stomping about in their shiny tall boots shouting awful things, but all our own soldiers are gone. It's as if they vanished in the winter fog. I'm afraid to walk out in the streets alone now.

Our own young strong soldiers are all at the front, we're told, but the trouble is no one knows where that front is, and in the meantime the Nazis here act as if they're in charge already. Just because they invaded

Denmark and Norway they feel they've won the war!

Churchill says we must not be cowed, the forces of good will win out at the end. I hope he's right.

What am I saying? He must be right. He must, he must!

Your friend,
Lara

New York, April 23, 1940

Most of my classmates are my age but taller. They seem older, so confident about their world, so sure of themselves. They are sure about everything, in fact. Their opinions ring out cold and clear as a Flemish church bell on a wintry Sunday morning.

I'm sure about nothing these days, not Belgium, not America, not myself. Least of all myself. I can't talk right. I'm slowed down with all that French and Flemish no one wants here. I can't say what I really feel because my English is too sketchy still. Clumsy, halting, riddled with mistakes, impossible. Will I ever be able to express myself in it?

L'Athénée Royale back home is beginning to look wonderful from this distance. Trapped by light little rules and large, tomblike silences, we banded together with plots to gag the teacher, or poison her, or pelt her with spitballs, and if none of that should do it to rebel or run away altogether. Under its conventlike appearance my school was a hotbed of plots and counterplots and quite exciting to be in, even if I hated it.

It's so different here. I can't tell teachers apart from

students. They wear the same bright clothes and laugh all the time. Everybody is so light and carefree, and everything, absolutely everything, is allowed! Fun is the password.

"Everybody in school is having fun, everyone but me, that is. Nobody even knows my name."

"Nobody knows your name; surely you didn't expect friendships so soon?"

Tante Elise's eyes dart back and forth, tick tock, tick tock, like a clock.

Uncle Jacques watches my fork scrape the food around the plate.

"You're not hungry, Elleke?" he asks, his gentle, worried eyes on me.

"Not really."

"No appetite, but it's not natural! Are you sick?"

"No, Tante Elise, I'm not sick. Just not hungry."

She looks as if she spit out some sour milk, she's so disgusted with me. "My cooking then?"

"No, Tante Elise, your cooking's good. I mean very good. I don't feel like eating, that's all."

I leave the table, knowing they'll talk about me and shake their heads.

New York, April 24, 1940

Yves is drumming again. The sound coming through the walls is a secret signal to me.

Yves's hometown is Antwerp. He lives upstairs with relatives as I do, and his parents are still in Europe as mine are, but he hasn't heard from his. Not since their passports were confiscated and they vanished. No one knows where they are now.

And so Yves drums and drums. Perhaps his drumming will reach his mother and father somewhere, perhaps.

But Yves isn't always sad. Sometimes his drums are funny and jumpy. I smear lipstick on my cheeks and do an Indian war dance and he chases me across the apartment with a mophead in his hair and we laugh until our bellies ache from laughing.

Sometimes we bounce to Dixie music. "A-men, A-men," we chant, along with the singers on the radio, "A-aa-men!" imitating the thick throaty voices. "Hold that tiger!" we sing, with Yves doing the *thump thump* of the tuba, his cheeks, puffed out chubby for the tubby tuba, while I clown on a make-believe trombone making rusty sounds.

Today is a special day. We're going to hear Gene Krupa play at the Paramount theater downtown. The place is jammed full with kids but hushed like a church. We are listening to Krupa softly beating his drums, slowly, softly, a little louder then. The drums are pounding faster now, fast and wild, wilder still, wilder and faster than the blood racing through us.

Bobby-soxers are jumping up in the aisles about us. My heart knocks hard against my chest. Something snaps and I let go. I'm clapping and shouting and singing along with Yves and everyone else.

We are changing, Yves and I, we are beginning to really hear that American beat.

New York, May 5, 1940

A letter from Maman today, hooray!!

Antwerp, April 25, 1940

Elleke mine,

We're leaving for Rio de Janeiro! Can you believe it? I can't, but our trunks are packed so it must be true.

Remember the tall man with the faraway look in his gentle blue eyes, Cousin Bernard, the Luftmensch? *Well, it was none other than Cousin Bernard, the adventurer, who lent us the two thousand dollars we needed to do-nate to the Brazilian Orphans' Association, and only then did Brazil welcome us as new immigrants.*

So it goes. Here the Flemish Nazis are growing, and not a day passes without some ugly incident against Jewish families now. There is terror in the air.

We must leave, we have no choice. It hurts to abandon our house; how many times have we had to drop our lives before? Never to see the old family photos clumped together cozily on the piano again, never to hear that scratchy gramophone with its sky-blue speaker . . . those Caruso records we used to sing to, the three of us!

Enough. This is not the time to cry.

Lovingly,
Your Maman et Papa

P.S. I'm taking the piano music, all of it; I cannot bear to leave it behind.

New York, May 10, 1940

NAZIS INVADE BELGIUM, HOLLAND, LUXEMBOURG BY
LAND AND AIR / DUTCH OPEN DIKES / ALLIES RUSH
AID / SITUATION CRITICAL

Germany struck another powerful blow at the
Western world today. Parachute troops made a
surprise landing before dawn in Belgium and bombs
blasted Brussels airport. The staccato of machine
guns could be heard above the anti-aircraft guns in
Antwerp, raising fears of many casualties.

Swarms of planes engaged in air fights over Am-
sterdam as well, and parachutists clad in Dutch uniforms descended at strategic points, occupying the
city. Holland promptly opened the dikes that are
part of her defense system.

At the same time Germany announced that Reich
forces had been launched against the Low Countries
to "protect their neutrality." Joachim von Ribben-
trop, Germany's foreign minister, declared that the
Allies had plotted with Belgium and Holland to attack Germany, compelling it to take corresponding
measures. "The time for settling the final account
with the criminal Franco-British leaders had come,"
he added.

New York, May 18, 1940

NAZIS PIERCE MAGINOT LINE INTO FRANCE / LOW
COUNTRIES BLITZED / BELGIUM, HOLLAND OVERRUN
IN WESTWARD SWEEP

The bold black headlines jump off the page. Belgium under the Nazis! What'll happen now?

It's a beautiful clear day here in New York. I look up at the sky, but the sky is blue and pitiless.

June 14, 1940

PARIS FALLS!

Photos of weeping Parisians, men and women both, watching Nazi troops march through the Arch of Triumph as France totters to defeat. More photos of Belgian, Dutch, and French refugees clogging the narrow roads with vehicles piled high with bedding, bikes, baby carriages, more bedding.

Where is everybody fleeing to? Where is there to go? What'll happen to those who stay behind?

The front-page text reads:

> Nazis Report Rout; Allies in Full Retreat as Swift Armored German Columns Sweep to New Successes. British Fall Back Behind Brussels in Orderly Retreat as Outer Fortifications of Antwerp Reached. Belgian Capital Moved from Brussels to Ostend on North Sea. Allies Admit Situation Grave. France's General Gamelin Issues Command: "Conquer or Die. The Fate of Our Country, Our Allies, the Destiny of the World Depends on the Battle Now Fought."

New York, June 15, 1940

"Elleke," Maman wrote on May 24th, "Elleke mine, we've just landed in Rio de Janeiro! We left May fourth —I cannot believe we got out six days before Hitler invaded us! A miracle, that's what it is, a miracle! Your Maman and Papa."

> Reich Tanks Clank on Paris' Champs-Elysées. Berlin Reports 100 Planes Bombed Britain.

"London bridge is falling down, falling down, falling down," the children sing, playing in my dark windy street here in upper Manhattan. "London bridge is falling down. . . ."

"National defense preparations were begun here in Washington," the paper says. "Roosevelt is busy."

> Eleven Days after Start of Offensive, German Thrust Reaches Channel and Stands Poised at England in Lightning War. Italy Declares War on Allies. Stab in Back, Declares Roosevelt.

"London bridge is falling down, falling down, falling down. . . ." I shut my windows so as not to hear the children. I cannot bear it.

"Elke is losing weight," I hear Uncle Jacques tell Tante Elise.

"Of course she's losing weight. She doesn't eat."

"She's upset," I hear him whisper to her. "She's uprooted. Lonely."

"Who isn't?" she whispers back fiercely.

I hate Tante Elise.

New York, June 30, 1940

Yves is in a rotten mood today. He is feeling down, I mean really down. He's sort of been that way ever since I got that letter from Rio, the one Maman dashed off when she and Papa first got there. He hasn't heard from his parents, not a word.

I did this stupid thing, too. I went up to him this afternoon and said, "Tell me something funny."

In the movies where I saw it done the heroine said it to the hero when he was in trouble and everything kind of straightened out. I thought it might work with Yves so I said it. But he just waved me away, so I guess it didn't.

I feel bad for him. He doesn't even drum these days, and drumming is what he cares most about. He sure doesn't like to talk much. Music says it all so much better, he says.

Even though we don't have long conversations Yves is still my only friend here, not counting Frau Braun. I've seen Ulli a couple of times but it's not the same as being with someone from your own hometown like Yves. Yves is special.

But just because he's my only friend here doesn't mean he's my boyfriend, you know. I don't like him that way, and me, I'm like a kid sister to him, that's all. He's fifteen and I'm thirteen and I'm just someone around because there's nothing better, see.

Still. I wish he'd get out of his rotten low mood, my friend Yves, because it's getting me down, too.

Rio de Janeiro, July 3, 1940

Elleke chérie,

I haven't the time to write to Jacques myself, running back and forth to the hospital the way I do every day, but please thank him for me. I know he means well—he's a good man, as good as they come—but tell him we don't need the money, we'll manage. We always have.

Papa's blood pressure is almost back to normal, and he'll be released from the hospital any day now, maybe as soon as next week sometime.

In the meantime we have some savings we can draw on, so don't worry about us.

We are so proud of your school marks! A B-plus in English composition. Pretty good for a newcomer!

We hug you, child,
Papa and Maman

Rio, July 15, 1940

Dear Elke,

I'm relieved to let you know that the heart attack Papa suffered was not severe. He's doing much better all the time. He can even have some salt in his food, so perhaps now he'll enjoy eating again.

Hurriedly, Maman

Rio, September 2, 1940

Elleke,

The beginning of spring here in this upside-down part of the world and things are looking up for us. Papa feels fine. He used his enforced rest to learn Portuguese—you should hear him speak—and, using the language, to make some connections to open a small import-export business. Rio suddenly looks gorgeous to us. If only there were some good news from Europe! Have you heard from anyone? I've had no news from my sister at all.

Lovingly,
Maman and Papa

New York, November 20, 1940

The letters from Europe are few and far between, but when they come their envelopes are brownish gray, with a red sticker across the top like a raw wound. OPENED BY CENSOR, the sticker says. The censors, of course, are Germans. My country has been occupied by them since May 10, 1940, when their Panzer units blazed through on their way to Holland and France. England is bombed every night but is free, still. The rest of Europe has collapsed. Scissors in hand, the Nazi censor sits astride the fallen continent, cutting its heart out.

Antwerp, November 29, 1940

Chère Elke,
   It is gray outside and always we are xxxxxxxxxxxxx xxxx. The nights are long now it's winter and we're very xxxxxx xxxxxx xxxxxxxxx xx. Everybody has xxxxxxxxx xxxxxxxxxxx it seems. It is only we xxxxxxxxxxxx xxx and xxxxxxxxxxxx who are here still.

Write. Please write.
Ginna

Antwerp, March 2, 1941

Elke!

This is not the xxxxxxxxx xxxxxxxxxx xxxxx *world you left. This is* xxxxxxxxx *world altogether. You would not* xxxxxxxxx xxxxxxxxxxxxxx *the things* xxxxxxxxx xxx xxxx *to people* xxx xxx xxxx xxx. *You would* xxx. *Life is* xxxxxxxxxxxxxx *now,* xxxxxxxxxxxxxxx *impossible.*

But we will xxxxxx xx xxx, *we* xxxx!

Please. A letter from you is our lifeblood.

Lara

Antwerp, April 16, 1941

Chère Elke,

Do you still remember your old friend Ginna? For me it is hard to remember anything from before the xxxxxx xxxxx xxxxxxxxxxxx *at all, there is* xxxxxxxxxxxxx *such* xxxxxxxxxxxx *things happening all* xxxx.

But even if you saw me you wouldn't recognize me, your fat friend, ha ha. I'm skinny now, very different from before. We're all different. We are xxxxxxxxx *now, and very* xxxxxxxx *all the time. There are still some things to laugh about, though, even if* xxxxx xxxxxxx xxx xxxxxxx *as before, but we try.*

And so I will not say adieu, I'll say au revoir,

Your friend always,
Ginna

New York, May 10, 1941

May 10, May 10, May 10, May 10, May 10, May 10, May 10, May 10, May 10, May 10, May 10, May 10.

]78[

Never will I forget that date. One year ago exactly they came in, the Nazis, and took over.

What is happening to everybody back home?

Antwerp, May 10, 1941

Elke!

Today, exactly one year ago xxxxxxxxxxx xxxxxxxx xxxx *came and took charge of our lives. Posters everywhere tell us what to do,* xxxxxxxxx xxxxxx *what not to do. Mostly what not to do.*

There is rationing for all the Belgians except for xxx xxxxxx xxxxxx. *Do we not get hungry like* xxxxxxxxx *else? No* xx xxxx xx xxxxxxxx xxxxxxxxx xxxx *scraps, if* xx xxx xxxx *them.* xxxxx xxx *turnips before* xxx xxxx xxxxx *quite good, really. As long as we're still* xxxxxx xxxxxxxxx *something, even if it's turnips, we're not* xxx xxxxxxx. *Some cannot go out in the fields to get them for themselves though, so* xxxxxxx xxxxxxxxxx. *Some are* xxxxxx.

I never see Ginna anymore. She seems busy, with what I cannot imagine.

Write quickly. There's not much time.

Lara

New York, August 12, 1941

Dear Ginna,

You never answered my last two letters—what's happening to you? Are you still in Antwerp, but too busy to write? Lara wrote how very busy you were, with what she did not know. Have you found war work? I am curious, please let me in on what it is you're doing!

I cannot imagine my round pretty friend skinny. Does that mean your curls are skinny now too, all stringy flat like mine? I cannot picture you like that. Please send me a snapshot to prove how skinny you are, eh?

But please, please write!

Elke

New York, November 6, 1941

Dear Lara,

Did you ever get that package of cocoa and salami and heavy socks I sent? There was coffee in it too, and a raincoat, but I never heard. And I haven't heard from Ginna at all. Is she still in Antwerp? Are you with your family? Where is everybody?

If only we could do something.

Your friend,
Elke

I seal the letter, knowing there will be no answer. It's gray out and I'm cold. Better go see Frau Braun, quick.

New York, December 7, 1941

PEARL HARBOR ATTACKED! Tokyo Bombers Strike at US Bases in Hawaii; Heavy Fighting Reported. US DECLARES WAR ON JAPAN "December 7, a Date Which Will Live in Infamy," says Roosevelt. December 11, 1941 / US NOW AT WAR WITH GERMANY AND ITALY AS WELL

America is at war; we're all in it now, the whole world. It is total war. At least it's not only poor battered Europe fighting Hitler, it's everybody. And we'll win, *we will*, WE WILL!

I hear Yves drumming war songs upstairs. "I'm coming up!" I shout, dashing out to be with him.

New York, February 9, 1942

I am fifteen today.

For some time now I've been feeling as if I am fifteen already, but maybe that's because I'm not flat up there anymore. It sort of gives me a different feeling, looking down on myself now. I mean it makes me feel up, sticking out like that.

Tante Elise and Uncle Jacques gave me this aquamarine ring for my birthday. I was so surprised I couldn't talk even though my mouth was wide open, and they laughed and said they found it in the snow with a tag on it that said Elke. I burst out crying then because it's so delicate and beautiful and I don't deserve it, especially after all the terrible things I've said about Tante Elise here in this secret diary.

Something else is making me feel pretty special too. I did something grown-up now that I'm fifteen. There is a lot of snow around but instead of spending the afternoon throwing snowballs I walked into this USO office and told them I was sixteen and wanted to help. USO is a kind of home away from home for soldiers. They looked at me and said, "OK, you can be a volunteer." So now I'm going to make sandwiches three times a week after school, and it really makes me feel part of America, doing something for the war effort at last!

Antwerp, May 10, 1942

Elke,

The date says it all. What's left xxxxxxxxxxxx xxxxxx xxxxxx *meeting* xxxxxxxxxxxxx *if we can still* xxxxxxxxx xxxxxxxxxxxxxxxx *our own conscience.* xx xxxxxxxxxx xxxxxxxxxxxxxxxxxxxxxxxx. *But even now* xxxxxx xxxxx xxxxxxxxxxx *choose.* xxxxxxxxx *for others* xxxxxx xxxx xxxxxxx *ourselves. That's what's left.*

Lara

November 8, 1942 / AMERICAN FORCES LAND IN FRENCH AFRICA / EFFECTIVE SECOND FRONT, ROOSE-VELT SAYS

"Nu ja," says Frau Braun. "Maybe we have come to a turning point in ze war?"

New York, November 11, 1942

This was the letter from Maman I found opened on Uncle Jacques's desk.

Rio, October 16, 1942

Dear Jacques and Elise:

Is it true what we hear, is it true they are deporting our people as slave labor to Germany and places un-known? We can't tell what's true and what's rumor down here, we are so isolated. But we cannot believe the

world will allow such barbarism against Jews. Your President Roosevelt, a good man, will not let this happen, surely?

Let us know what you hear, and thank you from my heart for being so good to our child.

Your devoted sister,
Deena

New York, February 9, 1943

Yves asked me to go see Fred Astaire tap dancing in the movies tonight and Frau Braun baked a chocolate cake for my birthday, but best of all was getting a letter from Papa and Maman today.

Rio, February 2, 1943

Elleke,

Happy birthday, sweet sixteen! My arms ache with a longing to hug you.

Did you have any news from Régine in Antwerp? (You'd think it would be possible to hear from one's own sister!) From anyone back home? Here in Brazil we hear nothing but the most frightful ugly rumors.

May your sixteenth birthday bring an end to this terrible war.

Hugs and kisses from Maman and Papa

Then there was this from Lara in the same mail. It is rare to get a letter from Antwerp at all any more, but some still trickle through.

Antwerp, February 1, 1943

Elke!

I heard some xxxxxxxxxxxxxxx xxxxxxx xxxxxxxxxxx things about Ginna lately. I heard she was a xxxxxx xxxxx against them and then I heard she was a plain xxxxxx xxxxxx! Then again it was said she xxxx for them, but no one is sure of anything.

But I simply can't believe that of her, can you? It is strange that she's not hungry when the rest of us are xxxxxxxxxxx, though. This last month no one's seen or heard from her. I'm afraid she too has been xxxxxxxxxxxx xxxxxxx but no one knows that either, or where it is.

Why don't you write, Elke? Don't you know it's the only xxxxxxxxx xxxxxxxxxxxxx left us here?

Lara

Antwerp, February 26, 1943

Elke! Elke!

They are taking xxxxxx xxxxxxxxxxx away! Can you hear me? The xxxxxx xxxxxxxx are gone, the xxxxxx xxxxx are gone, almost xxxxxxxx xxxxx is left. No one knows xxxxxxxx to, nor for how long. We are told better work xxxxxxxxx, concentrated xxxxxxxx xxxxx xxx xxxx but I don't xxxxxxxxx it for a minute. We've seen too much xxxxxxxxx to trust what the posters xxxxxx xxx.

I will not write again, I feel.

Is it possible it is xxxx xxxxxxx Elke? Is it xxxxxxxxxxx xxxx for us all?

Lara

New York, March 10, 1943

Midterms are coming. I'll have to skip my visit with Frau Braun today. Too bad. I'm flying all the way home from school to beat those biting, icy winds off the Hudson River. It's a bleak day in March, raw, cruel, the kind of day nothing good ever happens.

I'm at my desk, chewing my yellow pencil. Gritty gusts rattle the windows and distract me. The doorbell rings. Good, I'm not in a studying mood anyway. Mah-Jongg time already? But it's only three o'clock, far too early for the ladies. Zzzz, goes the buzzer. I dash to the door to open it.

"Charles!" I scream. "Charles? How, Charles? How?"

"I swam," he says.

"You swam! You swam?"

"My ship was torpedoed and American sailors rescued us. When we docked in New York Harbor I jumped ship and swam ashore, and here I am! But what's the matter, you think you're seeing a ghost?" Charles says, laughing.

I'm shaking all over, and sobbing. I hug him, laughing and crying and laughing. Charles's ghost feels very real. Charles in New York to see me! I steal a quick glimpse in the mirror to make sure it's really me and a flushed face grins back happily.

Later, washed and warm again, hands cupped about hot tea, feet in fresh socks up on the table, Charles talks at last.

"Was it bad, Charles?"

"Chaotic. Mass confusion is what it was. Of course

you know there is no Belgian army left, it's been routed. The soldiers are all gone: prisoners of war or missing." He smirks, suddenly: "I'm one of the missing."

My heart is thumping loud as I plunge, "What news of friends do you bring?"

The smirk leaves Charles's face. "Just before I left I saw Lara at an underground meeting she had organized. She'd worked very hard for it and seemed tired. She was coughing a lot. I don't know how she did it, she was so skinny, a bag of bones she was."

I shut my eyes. "And Ginna, what have you heard about Ginna?"

"Let's go outside for a breath of air," says Charles.

The wind slaps sharp at our faces as we go out. We don't talk as we go down my street and turn the corner onto Broadway, noisy with small children and mothers and overflowing shops.

"Just look at these bakery windows filled with whipped-cream cakes," Charles marvels. "I'd forgotten whipped cream still existed!"

I'm not going to ask about Ginna, I think, not just yet. "And Frans, he's still Antwerp's limping lamplighter?" I ask lightly.

Charles stops short. He takes my hand in his and looks hard at me. "Frans was shot," he says.

Charles hasn't understood me. "I mean Frans Verbeeck, my neighbor on De Korte Vandongen Straat. The Spanish Civil War invalid," I explain.

"Frans was shot."

"Shot?"

"For fighting against Franco in Spain, for being a Communist sympathizer. Flemish Nazis did it. Up against the wall in his own street."

My street, my street with Frans's blood on it. I'm going to throw up. I drop Charles's hand and run on ahead, the rain streaming down my face. Charles catches up and takes my hand again. "That's what war is, Elke. Ugly. At least he fought *against* them."

We walk on, oblivious to the trucks and traffic about us. "And Ginna," I finally ask, though somewhere I already know. "What about Ginna, Charles?" My insides tighten at the coming of bad news.

"Forget about Ginna," Charles says, his arms tight about me to protect me. "Ginna's a prostitute."

The blow lands below the belt. "No," I groan. "Oh, no, no no no—I don't want to hear, you hear?" I'm hollering, hollering to tear the pain out of my head. "Go away!" I shriek, pummeling Charles, hitting him, scratching him. I tear away from him and run, and run. Wind and rain howl with me as I run.

"Na, na, *Liebchen*," Frau Braun says when I come in to hide. "I bring hot tea *mit* lemon, *ja?*" She pats my hair. "You got wet outside because you had bad news from home, *nicht wahr?*"

She asks nothing more, says nothing more, but pulls up a chair beside me. We both sit and stare out at the fire escape in silence.

Later, much later, when I go out into the street before

coming home again, my apartment house looms dark in the night, its sooty windows streaked dirtier with rain by artificial light, and Charles has left.

New York, March 19, 1943

I did not see Charles after that.

I was awful to him. I was stunned by what he told me and I was awful to him, plain awful.

There was so much more I wanted to ask him, so much more I had to know, but now I can't find him anywhere. He must have joined a ship again and returned to Europe without ever calling me.

He left a tiny bottle of Carnet de Bal perfume hidden on my desk, but I never saw it till later. And now I can't even say thanks. It's my favorite perfume in the world, better than any Tante Elise has on her vanity table, even. It makes me feel like a real woman every time I take a whiff and dab some behind my ears, not like some silly sixteen-year-old who doesn't know how to behave when her friend from across the sea comes to visit.

Now he's gone. There's no one but Uncle Jacques and Tante Elise and me left. I think I must have dreamed up all the others. None of them ever existed. My past is some strange tale someone else made up for me.

New York, March 20, 1943

There are no more letters.

The war rages in Southern Europe, on the Eastern front in Russia, in Africa, in the Pacific. The whole world is in flames.

There are no more letters from home.

New York, April 20

A spooky thing happened today. A crumpled letter
Ginna came inside an envelope postmarked Lo
England, April 9, 1943.

Inside the English envelope were two letters
smooth and the other a wrinkled letter from Ginn;
had been straightened.

Here's what the smooth letter said:

London, April 9,

Dear Miss Colbert,

*I found this letter in a street in Antwerp. It
bunched up inside a shoe that had been tossed out
hurry, but because it had an address I flattened it
and am sending it on to you.*

Do the same for me some day.

Cheeri

Here's what the other one said:

Antwerp, April 2, i

*Maybe you better forget about me, Elke, forget
ever knew a girl called Ginna.*

*Some boys promised me chocolate and bread if I u
with them. Now when I get cigarettes or coffee or ch
olate I bring it home and no one asks where I got it
don't you*

"Don't you dare," was scribbled on the bottom, "you can't know what it's like, you'll never never know, never."

I crush the letter tight against my face and sob.

New York, April 21, 1943

There is no news from anyone. Europe is tearing itself apart in the war, but I'm just a schoolgirl going to classes. Young men have all been drafted into military service, but my classmates and I go about our daily doings as if nothing were the matter at all.

Every now and then something monstrous like a report about all the Jews in a village being locked inside a synagogue and set on fire by the Nazis hits the paper here. Or some item about fourteen-year-old partisans left dangling on gallows for weeks as a lesson to anyone planning to resist the Germans. Or a bulletin about an entire Jewish community rounded up and ordered to dig their own graves before being shot. But no one really knows anything. It can't be true, is what everyone says; just war news, exaggerated. Pure sensationalism.

There is no way of finding out what is going on. Overseas telephones don't work for civilians. European cities are blacked out and all communication is muffled. Whatever radio newscasts can be heard are nothing but Nazi propaganda.

Battle statistics and locations are printed in our papers, but nothing about people, nothing about the terror of torn-up families deported to Germany's labor camps against their will. Rumors are multiplying, of course, but

then they're just rumors. No one knows anything.

I go along with everyone else and pretend things are normal by acting as if they are. As if *acting* normal will force things to behave and *be* nice and normal again.

But nothing makes much sense anymore. I don't sleep well. A huge dog snarls and lunges at me in my nightmares. I wake up drenched in sweat and start thinking. That's the worst—the thinking—but I'm too scared to go back to sleep for fear of meeting the German police dog again.

It's a bad time. Luckily there is Frau Braun, though. Thursdays and Fridays I help with the baking. I find her sitting by herself staring out the window when I arrive, but in no time at all she's her jolly self again. We assemble the flour, sugar, and eggs and get busy. Soon all smells buttery and hot and good, and I forget about the vicious dog that pounces on me at night.

New York, May 4, 1943

More newcomers have come to school. The new immigrants are called refugees. Refugee, a name with the ugly sound of fear.

I don't hang around the refugees much. Their all-too-familiar French or German reminds me of the European world I left behind; a raw, bleeding world at war that frightens me. Their jumpiness reminds me that terrible things are happening there now, this very minute, to my own family and friends.

I don't want to be reminded. I don't want to hear about being hounded and humiliated; I think of Ginna and Lara then, and cannot bear it.

The refugees' jitteriness mirrors myself when I first came here such a long time ago. But too much that's unspeakable has happened there since. I've been spared and I'm not really like them anymore. I'm a different girl now.

Perhaps I should, but I don't want to huddle and whisper of Hitler. I'd much rather dance the lindy to the jukebox at the corner drugstore with the kids from school.

I want to forget, that's what. I want to be an American now. To be American is to be like everyone else. To be American is to know there is going to be a tomorrow and a day after tomorrow, and even a day after, and that is tremendous.

Sometimes I don't know what I am, a part-time American or a part-time refugee. Sometimes I don't know who I am at all.

New York, May 10, 1943

Tante Elise is taking me·to Carnegie Hall to hear Artur Schnabel play Beethoven sonatas today.

"May tenth is not a day to stay home and grieve," she said. "Let's listen to something beautiful to remember there are noble things left in the world."

Tante Elise and I are good friends these days. I help around the kitchen and fix up my hair now and she likes that, and she asks me about school and boys and I like that a lot, and mostly she's not picky and snooty and aloof as she used to be.

It must be that Tante Elise has changed now that she's going to have a baby. She looks soft now, and when I kiss her good night her cheeks smell of warm milk. She's my best friend, almost, but of course she'll never be like Frau Braun, who's the top best.

Frau Braun knows what it's like to be a teenager in America and have boy troubles. Even though she's forty-three she has a gentleman caller who comes to visit, and so she understands about that sort of thing, but poor Tante Elise, all she knows is the same old Uncle Jacques.

New York, June 3, 1943

I've been here over three years now. I ride the rumble seat in cars and do the lindy as neat and crisp as anyone in my class. I'm an American. My tastes are American, my clothes are American. I'm as American as apple pie. Why, I even speak like a native.

When asked about that clipped accent of mine I make up some fanciful tale about having grown up abroad—Belgium or some such little country—and people believe me. "That's adorable," they say. "Don't ever lose that accent!"

That foreign manner is sassy and classy, boys tell me, real cute. I'm cute too, they tell me. Europeans are charming, especially if they speak French, ooh la-la!

I like being told I'm cute. I don't blush the way I used to, all awkward angles and shyness. I smile and say thanks the American way, bold and matter-of-fact. I am an American now.

There are times when I'm not so sure.

September 9, 1943 / ITALY SURRENDERS!

New York, November 6, 1943

ARRIVING NEW YORK DECEMBER 15 DETAILS LATER
KISSES PAPA MAMAN

Maman and Papa are coming from Rio! I cannot believe it, I cannot, I cannot! I simply cannot believe it. I am beside myself with happiness and excitement. My parents, my own Maman and Papa, with me again! How fantastic! How singled out in good luck I am to have this happen in the midst of war—to have them back, my very own, to hug them, press them tight to me again. . . .

I jump up startled. My own parents, will they know me after these long years? I am beside myself with dread, suddenly. To them I'm Elleke still, the terrified almost-thirteen-year-old they left on the boat back then. But I'm not that Elleke at all anymore. I'm Elke now, sixteen and American through and through.

Am I not?

New York, December 15, 1943

Today's the day. December fifteenth, the day Maman and Papa are arriving from Rio de Janeiro. I'm so excited I keep dropping things. Uncle Jacques is so mixed up he calls Elise Elke and me Elise, and we're all giggling like idiots.

Dry the dishes, plump the pillows. The time on the kitchen clock crawls today, as if to spite us. And suddenly it's four in the afternoon, time to go! "We forgot flowers!" cries Tante Elise, frantic now.

We're here at the Idlewild International Airport observation deck. Waiting. Waiting. Any sound at all makes us peer up at the sky to scan it for the big silver bird. I've been to the bathroom four times, not counting the times at home.

Something shiny slithers across the horizon. There it is! The huge bird comes closer, swells enormous, and lands on cat's feet. People spill out of it. I spot a small woman with a determined gait that's oddly familiar.

"Maman," I shriek, "Maman, Maman!" as I run to her. But she's so little, Maman is, her hair smoky gray now, her face crisscrossed with thin, spidery lines. "Papa, where's Papa?" I'm in a panic. "Didn't he come with you?"

"He's coming." She laughs, her voice young and high as we embrace again. Papa's the last one out of the plane. He walks down the steps slowly, holding on to the railing as he does. My heart sinks. When did Papa have time to become so frail?

New York, January 14, 1944

We are together again. It's been four years since that tearful parting at the Antwerp docks. It feels as if that was in someone else's life.

"You're taller," they tell me tenderly. "You're a young woman now." There's awe in their manner, as if they can't quite understand how it could have happened to their own little girl without them.

There's ache and tenderness in what I do not tell them. And you, I do not say, the anxious years have not been kind to you, they are etched in the lines of your faces. Saddened, I smile brightly not to show my true feelings.

"We're one family again," I cry, hugging them tight to me.

We live together as before, but it's not the same. Instead of being in a narrow townhouse on an ancient cobbled street we're in a brand-new apartment in noisy Queens. Jackson Heights will be lovely and leafy this summer, but right now the wind coils up between bare branches and blows forlorn.

There is a gap between us. Time gone by lies in that gap, and separation and loneliness. And the war.

My energetic Papa has found work but even though he's back on the job he moves slower than before. He gets to the diamond-cutting shop later than he used to and comes home earlier. His hands clasped behind his back he walks, lost in dreams of another place, another time. Cautiously he walks, gingerly, as if stepping on eggs.

And Maman clings to me. To her I'm her twelve-year-old still, to be babied and protected still.

But I'm almost seventeen, bursting with things of my own I want to do. Like going to the corner drugstore for an ice-cream soda with a date. Or the movies, maybe.

"Do you know this Young Man?" Papa asks. "Is he from a Good Family?"

The way Papa says Young Man makes him sound like

an enemy. They don't approve of going out on dates at all, my parents, but I'm too grown-up to be tied down, too Americanized. And so they try to make sure the boys that call on me are "nice" and "from Good Families."

I am much too acclimated for Papa's and Maman's taste, so different from the little shy Flemish girl I used to be. But don't you see I'm about to be seventeen, don't you see I'm bigger, bubbling with energy, changed? I want to scream the difference. Don't you know being fretted over makes me feel I'm drowning, chokes me?

We are home listening to a Mozart trio on the radio when a sudden urge to run free in the bracing cold grips me. I cannot sit still another instant.

"I'm off to the drugstore, Ma."

Maman startles. "In the dark, child?" She fixes me over her bifocals.

"I need bobby pins to set my hair, Ma."

Papa climbs out of his deep easy chair with difficulty. "Shall I accompany you then?"

Dear, dear Papa, I think lovingly, you're so gentle and Old World, you do not wish me to walk alone in the dark.

"Thank you, Papa," I say briskly, irritably, "I'll manage fine."

I fly down the four flights of stairs and slam the door hard behind me. I need air and space, all to myself. I'm split inside myself these days.

New York, May 30, 1944

After more than a year, a letter from Europe came to-day. It must have been smuggled out secretly. Its post-mark is smudged, but I don't care, I don't care, I have a letter from Charles!

May 1, 1944

Ma chère Elke,

Today is lilies-of-the-valley day. Flowers are pushing up all about us with a promise of spring and fresh re-newal but they are lying, they are lying. Bitter winds are blowing bad tidings. The flowers are mocking us, it is a false spring we are having.

You may never see this letter. I am in a hiding place, safe for the moment, but I have to let you know what I know, and it is bad.

No one is left back home. Lara is gone. She organized a rebellion inside the concentration camp and was caught. She was running a fever and coughing blood but her raw courage gave others strength. She was brave, Lara was.

Ginna, I'm sorry I had to tell you about Ginna. It's rotten. The chocolates and cigarettes kept her going for a while but in the end she too was rounded up for the transport train to the East. She was starving, her family was starving—let us not judge her.

Somehow I came across the border and joined the partisans here. Wipe your tears and remember, we are fighting for us all.

Yours,
Charles

PS. Flowers are innocent, they cannot lie. Perhaps spring will really come, after all?

Charles's letter explodes in my face. The memory of my hometown is not a dull ache somewhere behind my eyes anymore, it is sheer horror.

I've stopped crying. The sun moved into my room while I chewed the last of my nails. I stare at my hands, my dumb powerless hands, clenched into fists as I slam them against the sunlit wall and look out the window. Down below, trees are budding in a soft green haze and children play contentedly. Spring is sweetening all over, but my friends have vanished.

"It's all false," I rant, "false! We're lulled here, lulled by spring's warmth while over there they're hounded, hunted down like—like—"

Alarmed, Maman looks in. "Enough child, enough. . . ." She shakes her head and goes out the door.

Lara was more brave than I, but Lara's dead and I'm alive. Why? Why?

And Ginna, poor frightened Ginna, gone too.

I try to understand. Ginna was not a heroine, Lara was. Yet they're both gone, equalized by death. As if what they did when they lived makes no difference anymore now that they're dead.

And for what crime did they die? What is this terrible war that is a war against Jews inside the other war? What is it, what is it?

Maman holds me tight. "Enough weeping, child, enough, enough."

"Charles is fighting in the Resistance," I whisper. "Is he still alive? Tell me Maman, is he?"

Maman does not dry my tears. She does not rock me like a baby, telling me all will come out right in the end. Instead she hands me the heavy-duty string required for tying overseas food parcels. "Help me wrap these packages," she says.

New York, June 6, 1944

ALLIED ARMIES LAND IN FRANCE / GREAT INVASION UNDER WAY

Communiqué from the Allied Headquarters of Expeditionary Forces: The invasion of the West has begun. General Eisenhower threw his combined U.S., British, and Canadian troops, backed by sea and air forces, into action for the liberation of Europe today. A parade of planes carried Allied invaders over Normandy in France, where they landed by parachute. Troops went ashore at Le Havre, Dunkirk, and Calais, and heavy fighting rages.

D Day, the long-awaited day that will turn the tide ing each other. Antwerp is the capital of Flanders and against them for sure! Today is D Day, a fateful day! Back to the newspaper:

In Italy the Allies' motorized infantry roared through Rome without pausing in its pursuit of fleeing Germans. Roosevelt hailed capture of Rome as "great achievement toward total conquest of Axis. One down and two to go," he said.

The hate our family and many new friends share against the enemy has turned into a passion for geography. Nothing is more thrilling than sticking pins in reconquered German territory. The pins are Allied flags.

August 2, 1944 / NAZI ROUT GROWS; GERMANS SURRENDER PARIS

October 26, 1944 / US DEFEATS JAPANESE NAVY, MANY SHIPS SUNK, ALLIES CUT UP FOE IN LOW COUNTRIES

January 17, 1945 / RUSSIANS TAKE WARSAW, KRACOW; ALLIES ADVANCE ON ST. VITH IN BELGIAN ARDENNES

March 25, 1945 / GENERAL PATTON CROSSES RHINE; NAZIS REPORT RUSSIANS ARE MOVING ON BERLIN

April 30, 1945 / HITLER DEAD! US ARMIES CLOSE IN ON BERLIN WHILE RUSSIANS BATTLE DIE-HARD NAZIS IN SMOLDERING BERLIN STREETS

New York, May 8, 1945

THE WAR IN EUROPE HAS ENDED! SURRENDER UNCONDITIONAL; V-E TODAY!

Germans Capitulate on All Fronts as Allied Russian, American, and French Generals Accept Surrender. Reich Chief of Staff Asks for Mercy While Victory in Europe Day Officially Proclaimed Today.

The most deadly war of all time is over, and we won. We won! The war itself is over. THE WAR IS OVER!

Times Square bursts with wildly cheering throngs who toot horns and fill the streets with fluttering scraps of paper. Loudspeakers blare out the news into the ears of thousands, and shouts of triumph and relief explode all over the country, all over the world. Schoolchildren, factory workers, bankers and housewives gather at street corners to pray. Some link hands to dance. Many weep.

Uncle Jacques and Tante Elise bring their baby to Jackson Heights to celebrate with us. We drink so much wine the world turns pink. Jacques and Elise take turns singing mad gypsy tunes to each other and smash their downed glasses at the wall.

"Bravo!" cries Maman, belting out a *kazatske* song in full voice, the flush in her cheeks high and hot. She claps her hands, crouches on her heels, kicks them out and dances a fast furious gypsy dance before flinging her drink at the living-room wall. "Bravo!" we shout above the sound of splintered glass. "Bravo, bravo!"

Papa dances quietly by himself. He dances a slow shuffle, a pensive look behind his smiling sad eyes.

Neighbors come in to share victory toasts with us then.

"You folks from over there must be real happy," the man next door says, refilling his glass. "Now you can go home again."

Home. Where is home? Is home where one's house is? Is there a house of ours still standing in Antwerp?

Antwerp, September 18, 1945

We're back in Antwerp, Papa, Maman, and I.

After we heard that our home had been headquarters for the Nazis and the area heavily damaged with buzz bombs during the Battle of the Bulge, we were allowed to find out what was left of it, if anything. We'd given up hope on the house itself. We don't plan to ever settle here again after all that's happened, but still—it *was* our house.

What we came back for was to seek out surviving family and friends. That was the real reason for returning.

Pain and grief lie ahead in our search, we know, yet there was this overwhelming need to try. We were afraid, but we had to see for ourselves. Considering, it's a wonder we came at all.

We are here now, and it's weird. It's like being in a strange land that's somehow very familiar. The landmarks are here, but everything else has changed. Antwerp's once-busy streets are empty now, its formerly bustling shops quiet, their glass storefronts smashed or shuttered down tight. Only the charred shells of burnt houses gape wide open.

Here is the square where Denise and I played jump rope after school, but where is Denise? Where is the rest of the Huysmans family?

We are strolling from our little hotel on the Zeebrugge Straat behind the old cathedral toward our house. The day is beautiful, blue and crisply clear, the kind of day when memories leap out of hidden places.

And Jan, where is he now? Jan had six fingers on each

hand and was the envy of us all for catching balls better than anyone. Now weeds grow amidst the rubble that was his house once.

DE KORTE VANDONGEN STRAAT, it says on the blue street sign, my street. Frans Verbeeck's house still stands, but the front of it's been blasted out. We can see the kitchen still, its linoleum ripped, the table in its usual place in the middle of the room with four empty chairs neatly around it.

Lara's house looks the same as before but a stranger steps out the front door. Maybe Lara's father has changed. "Mr. Heller?" I shout, "Mr. Heller?" The man pays no attention. Carefully he locks the door behind him—as if the house were his—and walks past us.

No one at all is in Ginna's house. We found Ginna's younger brother Henri standing across the street staring at it, though. Henri was at the Dachau concentration camp until last April when Americans liberated it, and knows nothing else. When Papa presses him about the time before Dachau he smiles briefly. "We had food for a time then," he says, his face blank. "That was when Ginna was still working."

Henri never looked at us while he talked, but if he had it would have made no difference. His pale hazel eyes are vacant, as if he had moved out a long time ago, the very life sucked out of them.

He turned around then, and went away without as much as saying good-bye. I watched him go. Henri does not walk like other people anymore. Shrunken, weightless almost, he grazes the sides of houses like a passing shadow.

We are facing our old house. Unbelievably, it is whole still, primly upright between two black holes on either side of it. It is narrower than I recall. Dingier somehow, skimpier, smaller, but it *is* our house. Or was, before the Germans.

The three of us are planted in front of it as in a trance. "Enough of this, Deena, your face is drained of color," Papa tells Maman after a while. "Let's go back to the hotel; we can all use some rest now."

Antwerp, September 25, 1945

Again we are standing in front of our house, staring at it transfixed as if we're looking at a ghost. But it's not a ghost, it's our own house we're looking at. Even the doorbell is the same, still hanging on the very same black iron chain I yanked every day of my life.

I must do it. I'm going to do it. I'm going to ring that bell. I pull the chain to my house, my own chain to my own house.

A lace curtain lifts; a maid with starched apron and cap comes to the front door.

"*Ja*, what'll it be?" she cries, small Flemish eyes darting suspiciously. I clear my throat, regret my impulse.

"Are Monsieur or Madame in, by chance? You see, my parents and I, we used to live here before the war," I explain sheepishly.

The maid shrieks, suddenly. "I'll call the gendarmes if

you don't leave this instant!" And slams the door in my face.

Papa looks strange. "Let it go," he says. "They have it now."

"The lawyer told us to forget it," says Maman. "We owed some mortgage payments on it still so we lost the house. Best forget it, child."

At dinner tonight Maman's eyes are red and puffy but we talk of other things. Let it go, forget it, forget it.

It would have been easier not to come back here at all. Forget the past, paint it black the color of mourning and shut the door. Paint it gray like mist, paint it smoky the color of forgetting and be rid of it at last.

Antwerp, October 10, 1945

No one is left in Antwerp, it seems. Papa's cousin Josef is gone. His two young cousins who fought with the Belgian army were killed at the front early in the war. Albert died in a tank battle with the invading Germans in May 1940 and Léon was hit by an exploding grenade in the same week.

Maman's sister Régine, her husband and two children, are gone. Mevrouw Hoog remembers she had her infant and the brass Sabbath candlesticks in one arm and held on to her older child with her other hand when the Nazis took them away in 1942. But not one of them has been seen since.

Maman does not believe that her sister and family are gone for good. Every day, at five sharp when the train from Germany pulls in, she stands in the railroad station waiting for it to bring Régine back. It never does. The train straggles in late and half empty, and everyone getting off is always a stranger, but still Maman stands there and waits.

Mevrouw Hoog and her entire family are all here, but then they are Catholics. They had only one war against them to get through, not two as Jews did, so they had a chance.

I can't wait to leave this hateful, mangled Antwerp screaming with absence.

But there's more grim work ahead. We must find out about everyone still. We've been to the Joodsche Gemeente here on Jacob Straat, the Jewish Community office in charge of matters relating to present and former Jewish residents of Antwerp, and Papa has traveled to the Communauté Juive à Bruxelles as well. Both organizations have soup kitchens and provide sorely needed clothes and medicines to the few Jews left here, and both keep track of survivor records.

The building in Antwerp is war battered and shabby. Upstairs the records office has a sign on the door that says HOLOCAUST. A large chart is tacked to the wall. The facts, hand printed in block letters on it, make my blood stop.

> May 1940: 100,000 Jews live in Belgium: 55,000 in Antwerp, 35,000 in Brussels, 10,000 scattered in Charleroi, Liège, Namur.
>
> 1940–1942: Many Jews flee Nazi-occupied Belgium; no count exists.

September 2, 1942: The first of many convoys of Jews to Germany begins.

July 1944: 25,631 Jews have been deported in 31 transport trains. No Jewish children, women, or men are left in Belgium.

September 1945: 1244 Jews have returned.

I stand in front of the chart hoping to shield it from Maman. Mr. Kaufman, who runs the office, looks oddly familiar. Then I remember: Martin Kaufman, Antwerp's own man-about-town, handsome, devastating with the ladies. His steely-blue eyes are weary now, his blond hair faded and thinning.

Papa is incredulous. "Of all people, you, Martin, running an office such as this?"

"Felt I should help," says Martin briskly. "The least I could do."

Papa looks at him.

"See this?" Martin points to his hair. "This yellow mane made me pass as Flemish, so I forged false Flemish papers to go with it and spent the war working as a dockhand right here, *et voilà*. But you were looking for somebody. Name, please?"

"Berenson," says Maman, her face white. "Régine and Arthur."

Martin runs down a list with his forefinger. "You know the news on survivors is bad."

"How bad?"

"I'm afraid I see no Berenson here," Martin says.

"How bad?" repeats Papa, as if he didn't hear.

"As far as we know the odds of anyone escaping or even living through a Nazi death camp are slim."

"You mean concentration camp," says Papa then, speaking slowly, "you don't mean death camp. You don't, do you."

Martin's astonishingly blue eyes are fixed on us. "The war has only just ended; it's too soon to give up hope."

"Did you say death camps?" says Maman.

"Nazi concentration camps changed during the war, Mrs. Colbert. Some remained slave-labor camps, others were turned into factories for the purpose of murdering Jews. Camps such as Auschwitz, Dachau, Belsen, Treblinka, Maidanek . . . Mrs. Colbert. Mrs. Colbert!"

Maman clutches at Papa. "No," she groans, "God could not have allowed it, it can't be. No, no, no . . ." We are crying, even Papa is openly crying.

But no tears will ever hold this sorrow. Nothing can ever cover the enormity of this sorrow and grief. Nothing.

New York, November 5, 1945

A stack of letters waits for us on our return, some of them from abroad. They are brownish gray as before, and thin, but no red OPENED BY CENSOR stickers foul them.

Brussels, September 8, 1945

Dear cousins!

Do not doubt there are good people left in this world. Deep in the dead of war our Walloon friends the Massons came to take us to their farm here in the south of Belgium. What they did to save us was at the risk of their own lives.

Here we worked as farmhands in the fields through the four long years and managed to come through the nightmare.

There were bad times, more than we care to remember. Like the nights the countryside was searched with police dogs, and we were almost found. But we will not burden you with stories. Suffice it to say we are here and have some days left to live.

Your Gisèle and Marcel

P.S. Uncle André spent the war years hidden under a pile of straw high up on the chimney. Perhaps you recall that he is the dark-haired one among us blonds and too easy to spot therefore. Thank God we can laugh again and call him "André the stork."

Paris, September 12, 1945

My cousins,

From Genève, where we were fortunate enough to be all through the war years living from hand to mouth on whatever we could get from selling the old oil paintings, we finally made it back home to Paris—but what a changed Paris it is! Dreary, sad, trampled upon, but still our beloved Paris.

Our son Alex has come home again. We did not know where he was for two years but now we understand. Fighting with the underground—the French maquis—his whereabouts were secret. The stories he tells us! Derailing German train tracks, dynamiting German bunkers, sabotaging the Germans wherever, whenever possible, even to the point of pouring sugar into concrete mixers. That he was not caught is a miracle!

Now we start all over again. We have nothing left but our lives, but that is more than most.

Our best wishes,
Monique and Max

P.S. I wish we had kept some of those oils we sold. We're told Chagalls fetch a lot of money now!

Moscow, September 22, 1945

Cousins,

You don't remember me, I'm sure. I'm the cousin who chose to go to the USSR because humanity's future depended on it. Here is where a doctor like myself could be truly useful, I thought. The burden of the world rested with idealists like me to make it better.

How sadly mistaken I was. A pediatrician was not needed just then. Iron and lumber were. So I was sent to a labor camp in Siberia, where I cut timber at way below zero, when winds howl and bite like wolves, and lived on thin grass soup. If you can call that living.

I will say that Siberia cured my delicate stomach, however. I can eat anything short of tree bark and stay healthy. To think my mother worried over my sniffles and babied me with camomile tea at the slightest cold— ironic, isn't it? That I should have survived when strong ones perished. Who is to say for whom the bell tolls?

From Monique in Paris I heard that your entire family got to the Americas just before Hitler invaded Belgium. You escaped, as you Americans say, by the skin of your teeth. Luck! Some have it, some don't.

I read my letter over. Just because the war is over I must not take survival for granted. Not yet I shouldn't. Little Father here is watching over us. Perhaps I should learn to pray even at this late stage.

Yours,
Ida

P.S. We could use warm clothing if you can spare any. Socks, scarves, sweaters, anything and everything. Moscow nights are harsh.

Buenos Aires, October 4, 1945

Dear family,

We are brother and sister, children of your late brother Walter, may he rest in peace. Never mind how many there were; only we two are left.

We are here because we threw ourselves from a moving cattle train filled with people like us. The train was heading east at a fast clip; we had been going three days without a drop of water. It was getting dark. The guard left to smoke a cigarette and we leapt past him into the fields. He shot at us but missed. You might say we are back from the dead.

I broke my ankle from the fall but Minka set it with my shirt sleeve. We wandered all through the night, but late next morning when the sun was high we found a drinking well at last. It was there a kind nun found us. The convent took us in, fed us, educated us, and, forgive us, baptized us.

Though we are practicing Catholics we have not forgotten our dear family. We heard that a part of the western branch had survived the massacres and was living in Paris and New York. We are yearning for contact. That is why we found your address and are writing you.

Your cousins,
Mendel and Minka

P.S. Our names are María and Manuel now. We work hard for our daily bread here in Argentina. I am a maid and my brother is a carpenter's helper, but we manage. Do not think we are writing to ask for help.

Copenhagen, October 10, 1945

Cousins mine:

An air raid saved me from the gallows. I was up on the scaffolding, the rope dangling around my neck, when suddenly the bombers appeared in the sky out of nowhere. American planes they were, bless them! Minutes later the bombs exploded and set the camp ablaze. It was beautiful. The screaming and confusion! It was beautiful.

In the midst of the yelling and chaos I felt peace. The rope still about my neck, I began to laugh. Such laughter, the tears scratched trenches in my stubbly cheeks. When I stopped laughing I saw that all those who hadn't died from the explosions had gone. It was getting dark.

Someone moaned nearby. It was my friend, the only one I cared about in that concentration-camp hell. Blood was gushing from his arm. The rope around my neck came in handy. I tied it above the wound, slowed the bleeding, and saved his life. It was then I decided to become a medical aide—but more of that later.

Bundles of rags though we were, we made our way here. Danes are the best, the most humane people in the world, but I still want to leave and come to the USA. All of Europe smells of death to me.

One favor. Send immigration forms here to me, but please no money. I am self-supporting and in good health, if underweight. I thank you.

Bernard

Bruxelles, October 11, 1945

Mlle. Colbert,

Lara and I were at Belsen concentration camp together but only I survived. It should have been the other way around because of what she did for others, but there is no justice. If there were, would Dachau and Treblinka and Auschwitz and Belsen death camps have existed?

Lara organized storytelling in the camp. She did it to make the children forget their fears and help their mothers forget theirs for a while. She saw to it that our stinking watery soup rations went to the weakest first, and when they were too sick to stand she propped them up so they wouldn't be shot on the spot. Sometimes she hid them behind those who had died during the night, giving them just a little more time to stay alive.

And then they took her away, and it was all over for her.

I wanted you to know about Lara. I am proud that she was my friend, too.

Sincerely,
Suzette Berger
12, rue Waterloo, Bruxelles

Jerusalem, October 15, 1945

Elleke!

Can you hear me, Elleke? It's me, Charles, calling you!

It was a dark time when I last wrote to you. I was in a dank cave in the Vosges Mountains with the partisans in France—what a time it was. We never knew if we'd live to see the next day. We'd fled from Paris, where we were wanted for printing an underground newspaper and plastering anti-Nazi posters all over the city, and now busied ourselves sabotaging rails and blowing up ammunition dumps. We were hunted with police dogs, but they never found us.

How did we do it? Somehow—and this may seem hard to believe, Elleke—somehow the terror of those days was lit up with sunlight. Danger and hunger are nothing in the face of stopping evil. And we were so close to one another, that ragged tattered band of us, it was as if we partisans had one skin.

Do I sound nostalgic for the bad times? Maybe I am, I don't know. Things were simpler then. There was wrong and right, or black and white, and it was clear which was which.

In due course I became a paratrooper behind enemy lines and fought openly. Became a hero, decorated. Linked up with a British unit in Africa to fight pro-German Arabs, landed in Palestine, and this is where I am. When will you join me, Elke?

Ever yours, Charles

New York, November 6, 1945

I dream of Ginna.

The moon sits on the roof of my house in Antwerp and lights up the street. Ginna is standing on the corner licking a lollipop. "What are you doing a silly thing like that for?" I cry, but in answer she only laughs, her eyes hollow in her baby face.

I dream of Lara.

A cold wind is howling through the tent flaps where Lara is dishing out soup to starving inmates. "Your share," she says, "but hurry, hurry." She comes closer, her blue eyes burning in the dark as she moves toward me. I rear back, terrified.

Suddenly Lara is above Antwerp's zigzag rooftops, climbing fast. I run after her, but she runs faster and vanishes in the clouds. I claw at the clouds trying to get at her, and wake up.

At dawn I'm still awake, trying to unscramble myself. Had I stayed there, could I have become like Lara, helping others with raw, desperate, selfless courage? Or would I have been like Ginna, driven by hunger and terror to save only myself?

Do you choose? Or does it simply happen to you?

I try to make sense out of senselessness. I would so have wanted to be a Lara, but could I have done it? In the end, do I have it in me?

I don't know. I don't know, I don't know. . . . Never will I know.

Atlantic Beach, N.Y.
November 17, 1945

I pit myself against the foaming sea here where I've come to find an echo. A raw wind whips the hair about my face. I scream my anger and grief at the waves, I rant till my voice is hoarse. The boiling sea rages louder than I.

I run till I sink down on the beach, panting. I don't belong anywhere, I think—neither here nor there. Not over there where those I loved who felt and spoke like me are no more. Not here where the English words still sound new and odd to me, where the different ways still seem strange.

The greenish sea roars; surf lashes the wet sand. And yet . . . Papa and Maman are here with me now, I have some new friends here at last. This country is good to me—can I make it mine?

Calmed, the little waves lap at the shore and leave. In and out, monotonous as breathing, they come and go.

My eyes heavy with weeping, I watch the tide go out. The ocean is stilled at last, spent as I am.

Survivors are surfacing here and there, scattered all

over the world. Painful beginnings in new, foreign places. Damaged people, torn up and transplanted, they will yet take root. Who knows, flower. Yes, flower.

Maybe I will too? Maybe I, too, belong? Not only there or only here, but to myself?

The ocean is magnificent. It is emerald streaked with turquoise. It is deep purple shot with greens and blues. It is black and pale pink with navy patches and keeps changing. The sea smells of the deep, yet the salty air feels fresh, and alive.

Anne Rose was born in Antwerp, Belgium, and lived there until she came to the United States during World War II. *Refugee*, her first novel, is based on her own experiences. She is already known as the author of several award-winning picture books, and is currently working on her second novel.

Ms. Rose was graduated from Hunter College and did postgraduate work in psychology at Columbia University. She was at one time an artists' representative in San Antonio, Texas, and later ran an art gallery in Connecticut. The mother of four grown children, Anne Rose lives with her husband in Rowayton, Connecticut.